CHRISTOPHER WILLIAM BRADSHAW ISHERWOOD was born in England in 1904, briefly attended Cambridge, and briefly studied medicine. His first novels, *All the Conspirators* (1928) and *The Memorial* (1932), have been praised for their literary brilliance, but it is for his "Berlin novels," *Mr. Norris Changes Trains* (1935) and *Goodbye to Berlin* (1939), the basis for the highly acclaimed musical *Cabaret*, that he is most famous. During the same years, he collaborated with W. H. Auden on a number of plays: *The Dog Beneath the Skin* (1935), *The Ascent of F6* (1937), and *On the Frontier* (1938).

Mr. Isherwood left Europe in 1939 and came to California where he wrote Hollywood screenplays and his later novels—*Prater Violet* (1945), *The World in the Evening* (1954), *Down There on a Visit* (1962), *A Single Man* (1964), and *A Meeting by the River* (1967). He became an American citizen in 1946 and settled in Santa Monica where his friendship with Aldous Huxley inspired the religious pursuits that have become an important part of his life. He is today a student of Vedanta and has written extensively on various aspects of Hindu philosophy. In recent years he has been active as a guest lecturer and visiting professor at distinguished universities, and has become an increasingly active supp

Other Avon books by
Christopher Isherwood

A MEETING
BY THE RIVER

CHRISTOPHER ISHERWOOD

 A BARD BOOK/PUBLISHED BY AVON BOOKS

Drawing of Christopher Isherwood by Don Bachardy.

AVON BOOKS
A division of
The Hearst Corporation
959 Eighth Avenue
New York, New York 10019

Copyright © 1967 by Christopher Isherwood
Published by arrangement with Farrar, Straus and Giroux
Library of Congress Card Catalog Number: 78-61556
ISBN: 0-380-37945-7

All rights reserved, which includes the right
to reproduce this book or portions thereof in
any form whatsoever. For information address
Farrar, Straus and Giroux, 19 Union Square West,
New York, New York 10003

First Bard Printing, November, 1978

BARD TRADEMARK REG. U.S. PAT. OFF. AND IN
OTHER COUNTRIES, MARCA REGISTRADA, HECHO EN
U.S.A.

Printed in the U.S.A.

To Gerald Heard

1

Dear Patrick,

    I suppose you'll be surprised to hear from me after this long silence—almost as surprised as I should be to hear from you. We seem tacitly agreed on one point at least, that there's no sense in exchanging letters just for the sake of chatter. I know you're a very busy man and I shouldn't dream of bothering you, if a situation hadn't arisen which threatens to become awkward.

    Yesterday I got a letter from Mother telling me that you're in the United States on business and that you may be going on from there to some part (unspecified) of southern Asia. She ends by saying wouldn't it be nice if you were able to come to India and visit me.

    Of course this may be just Mother's usual vague talk. She is utterly vague as always, says you're in Los Angeles but doesn't give your address there, which is why I'm sending this letter to your home address in London, to be forwarded. She doesn't even seem to know what this business of yours is. Ordinarily I'd take it for granted that it was to do with your publishing firm, but do they publish books in Los Angeles? Didn't you once tell me that that was all done on the East Coast? And southern Asia sounds even more unlikely. However, I'm probably out of touch with the march of progress in this as in so many other ways. I certainly have no wish to pry into your affairs.

    I'm only writing because of a stupid misunderstanding which has now got to be cleared up without further delay. I admit I was responsible for it in the first place, though I must say I don't see why I or anyone else should be expected to account for his actions to people they don't really concern. The point is, Mother is still under the impression, and I suppose you and Penelope are too, that I'm here working for the Red Cross in Calcutta, just as I actually was working for them in Germany, up to a year ago. Well as a matter of fact I'm not. I'm in a Hindu monastery a few miles outside the city, on the bank of the Ganges. I mean, I am a monk here.

I won't bore you with the whys and wherefores of all this. I doubt if they could possibly interest you. I'm well aware that my reasons for doing what I've done must seem hopelessly subjective and personal to anyone looking at them from the outside. In any case, reasons cease to be important as soon as a decision has been made that can't be altered. In a little more than two months from now I shall be taking my final vows.

I simply want to ask you a favour. It's a big one, I know. Will you tell Mother about this for me? I have let things slide so long that it has become almost impossible for me to tell her myself. From me she'd expect a lengthy explanation and that would involve me in all kinds of oversimplifications and rationalizations in order to make her understand, or imagine she understood. Whereas the very fact that you know almost nothing about the situation should make it relatively easy for you. I'm not asking you to tell any actual lies, but it would be good if you could make her feel that I haven't done anything so very outlandish or extraordinary from your point of view, and that you know I'm all right. Assure her that I'm in perfect health, which is true, and getting enough to eat. The food here is absolutely adequate, though perhaps not by her standards. Those are

8

the only two things she really cares about. If you can manage to reassure her somehow then she'll soon lose interest in the whole business. You always used to be so clever at calming her down and getting her to accept accomplished facts.

Sorry to be such a nuisance.

Don't bother to answer this.

Oliver

My Dear Oliver,

well, of course this is a tremendous surprise. It's something one simply can't react to quickly—except by saying, which I hope you take for granted, that I wish you well with all my heart in your great new change of direction. It would be impertinent of me to claim that I understand, even dimly, what made you do it. How could I? I just have to trust your judgement and believe that you've done what you had to do and followed your vision of the truth to its logical conclusion.

I don't want to embarrass you, but I feel that this is the right moment to tell you I have always admired you enormously, far more than perhaps you realize. (In fact I'm willing to bet you don't realize it at all!) When we were both boys, I must have seemed to you a very usual, cold and stand-offish sort of elder brother, part of an Establishment against which you naturally rebelled. I was probably stuffier than I shall ever be again in my life, and in a way older; when I look back on that public school persona of mine nowadays I feel positively juvenile by comparison! And, alas, I know only too well that I brought that persona with me whenever I came home. Throughout the holidays I remained a prefect, acutely conscious that you were both my junior and A Junior. If we'd been at the same school—thank God we weren't!—I'd have had the power to order you around and even beat your backside with a cane. No doubt I asserted myself all the more because you were a good deal bigger than I was, even then. I am sure I greatly resented that, though I would never have admitted it!

I think you'll agree that my attitude did change, after we grew up. I know I did my damnedest to make you feel that it had. If I didn't altogether succeed, it was because I was secretly in awe of you, which made me shy and sometimes tactless. You always appeared to be so strong and self-sufficient. You made no compromises. You didn't even seem to know there were any compromises one could make! You felt a call to do something—your friends The Friends call it a 'concern' if I remember rightly—and so you went straight ahead and did it. As I watched you, I couldn't help feeling awfully corrupt and shop-soiled, because I'm so different.

But it's really a waste of time, apologizing for the Past. Let's look ahead! You know, there's one great advantage that you and I have now—that it's been such an age since we last saw each other, more than six years! So when we do meet again—if we ever do!?—we should be able to talk to each other pretty objectively. Any little frictions we may have had will have become unimportant. I can only speak for myself, of course, but I know that's how I shall feel.

Naturally I'll do my best to reassure Mother, as you ask me to. But, Oliver, I must say you don't give me much to go on! I know there are aspects of your new life which I couldn't hope to understand, and you are right not to even try to explain them to me. I do protest, though, against your assumption that I'm not interested in what you call the whys and wherefores. I am *deeply* interested, and on my own account quite as much as on yours.

It would help me enormously with Mother if you

wouldn't mind answering just these four questions (very crude ones, I'm afraid, but bear with me!): How did you come under the influence of your new beliefs? How long ago did it happen? (Not very long, I assume, since I know you've only been in India a year at the most.) You speak of taking your 'final vows'. Will that mean that you'll then become incommunicado? Is there any hope of our ever seeing you again in England?

If you could scribble some kind of answers on a postcard, no matter how brief, I should at least know better how to break the news. But if you prefer not to, I shall respect your silence, of course. And if I don't hear from you I'll cope with the situation as well as I can, relying on my (not inconsiderable) powers of invention!

And, dear Oliver, I can't tell you how glad I am to have had at least this word from you. As you rightly say, we are neither of us very communicative. But perhaps I might add in self-excuse that Penelope and I stopped writing because we honestly felt you didn't want to be bothered. I must remind you that you paid two or three visits to England during those years you were working over in Munich. No doubt you were on Red Cross business and pressed for time. Still, you managed to travel all the way up to Chapel Bridge and see Mother. But you never once looked us up while you were in London, or even telephoned!

Affectionately, as always,
Patrick

Dear Patrick,

thank you for your letter. It makes me feel I owe you an apology. I see now how cold and superior my letter must have sounded. It was insufferable of me to write to you in that tone, and at the same time burden you with telling Mother. My curtness and rudeness were due to the fact that I felt terribly embarrassed to be asking you to do this for me. When you wrote back so nicely, I was ashamed. It's obvious that I at least owe you a proper explanation, in place of that ultimatum, and now I'll do my best to give you one, though it won't be easy. No, of course I didn't really think you wouldn't be interested! I only said that in self-defence.

The first thing I have to correct is your quite logical supposition that my decision to become a monk is something very recent, made since my arrival in India. Which would mean that it was an impulsive, not to say hysterical act, prompted no doubt by the influence of the Mysterious Orient! Anyone who knows Hindu religious life will be able to assure you that I couldn't conceivably be taking my final vows within a year of becoming a monk, at least not in any reputable monastic order. But how could you be expected to know that?

No, this isn't a recent decision, or an impulsive one. The whole thing started long ago. In fact, it had already started when I last saw you all in England in 1958. If you remember, I'd been offered the German job through the International Red Cross in Geneva, and I'd flown on from there to interview the people in the Munich office about it and had then decided to take it.

It was while I was in Munich that first time that I got to know a Hindu monk who'd been living there for some years. He'd formed a small group who used to meet with him several times a week to practise meditation and study Vedanta philosophy. I ran across this monk quite by accident—as it then seemed to me, anyway—in a public library, and we began talking. Something about him fascinated me, from the first moment; it was his very quiet unemphatic air of assurance. What I mean is, nearly all the other people who had ever struck me as having great assurance were also self-assertive and complacent, in fact downright stupid. So I felt I was meeting a new sort of human being, almost. He wasn't at all impressive physically. He was small and frail and skinny, with untidy grey hair cut rather short, and he can't have weighed much more than a hundred pounds. He was in his middle fifties but looked older, except that his eyes were young, very clear and bright.

He had, as I say, this extraordinary calm assurance, without being in the least aggressive. It was I who was aggressive—as you may well imagine, knowing me! When I found out in a general way what he believed, I told him without making any bones about it my opinion of people who try to save their own souls while neglecting the ills of their neighbours' bodies. That was how I saw the human situation then, and it seemed awfully simple to me. You only had to choose between social service and private selfishness. The very idea of mysticism set my teeth on edge—I was even privately critical of the Quakers because they wasted valuable work-time on their silent periods—and *Hindu* mysticism seemed the last straw!

I can see clearly now, looking back, that my attitude was too simplified to be absolutely sincere and that I wasn't nearly as sure of it as I imagined I was. If you do the kind of work I'd been doing, you keep getting your nose rubbed in the fact that for millions of people in many parts of the world life is basically hell. Sometimes the sheer horror of this blots out everything else, and your efforts to do something about it seem futile and idiotic and almost indecent, a form of self-indulgence. What's the use of it all, you think. Aren't I merely using these wretched people to salve my own conscience? I had been through quite a few of these bouts of desperation myself, but I had always got over them by working extra hard and then tried to forget them altogether.

So perhaps I was actually less unwilling than I real-

13

ized to be receptive to this strange little man. Anyhow, as we went on talking, he somehow made me start questioning the very thing I thought I was most certain about, my work and why it was worthwhile. I began defending it even though he wasn't attacking it, and whenever I found I couldn't make my defence hold water I looked at him in dismay and he smiled!

I don't mean, of course, that all this happened the first time we met. It's impossible for me now to remember our conversations separately, because they were really all parts of the same conversation, which kept being dropped and picked up again and wandering backwards and forwards and repeating itself in different words. Also, as far as I was concerned, it was more than a mere conversation. It was a confrontation with this individual who, just by being what he was, intrigued and mystified me and undermined my basic assumptions as no one else had ever done before.

We talked, that first day, until the library closed, and then he asked me to come and see him next morning and I did, and after that we spent several hours together every day until I absolutely had to cut my stay in Munich short—the Red Cross people were getting impatient, I'd already been there two weeks longer than was planned—and hurry over to England to settle things up so I could return to Germany and start work.

You're probably beginning to understand why, when we were together in London, I didn't tell any of you anything about the Swami. (That was what we used to call him in our group, it's the usual title of a Hindu monk who has taken the final vows, just as you say Father to a Catholic priest. The Swami had a Sanskrit name, as they all do, but if I were to use it here I know it would only make him sound that much stranger and more foreign to you, which is exactly what I want to avoid.)

I was still greatly disturbed by my meeting with the Swami, and correspondingly defensive. I still wasn't at all sure what I really thought of him and his attitude to life, or how I was going to react to it. So the mere idea of describing him to anyone else embarrassed me to the point of panic. I was afraid of being laughed at, of course—most of all by Penelope, because in those days she was quite a devotee of Vedanta philosophy, not to mention Zen Buddhism and Meister Eckhart. (Is she still, I wonder?) There was a time when she used to get very indignant with me because of my lack of enthusiasm for such matters. She once told me I was a hopelessly intolerant arrogant materialist!

So I returned to Munich without revealing my secret and started in at the Red Cross job, and I wrote and told Mother how interesting the work was, which was true or at any rate only a half-lie. It would have fascinated me under ordinary circumstances, that's to say if I hadn't met the Swami. As it was, I often got the feeling that it was almost meaningless, because this other part of my life seemed so much more real. I loathe the way people use that word 'real', especially in religious circles, but here I mean it literally. During the hours when I was at the Red Cross headquarters everything seemed a bit dreamlike. Whereas when I got back to the Swami's room and sat down quietly with him—he often sat a long time without talking, which was disconcerting at first, but I got used to it—it was like coming out of a daze and asking myself, 'Where was I, all day long?' and then answering, 'I don't know exactly, but this is where I am when I'm awake.'

A few weeks after I got back to Munich, I moved in with the Swami. Before that, he had been living alone, which wasn't good at all because he had no idea of looking after himself. The members of his group were really devoted to him and they did their best, but they were all poor and they had to work hard to make a living. If they invited him to meals or brought him food, he would eat, otherwise he was apt to forget to do it. He had a quite nice though extremely small flat, but there was very little money left over when the rent had been paid. He was absolutely dependent on what we could afford to give him and he always refused to take anything more than was barely necessary. To make matters worse, his stomach was delicate and his heart wasn't functioning properly, in fact he had a poor constitution altogether. 'I have a Bengali body,' he used to say, 'not good for much!' He was astonishingly cheerful about it. And I never felt he was just keeping a stiff upper lip. He actually did seem to find his inefficient body, and the predicament of being obliged to live inside it, funny!

So I began cooking proper meals for him and doing the various jobs that needed to be done. It seemed odd to me at first, being in this relationship to an older man—partly, I suppose, because Father died when we were both so young, partly because I'd never lived with only one other person before, but always in institutions and communities, or by myself. The Swami took it quite for granted, however. And soon he began referring to me as his 'disciple'. To begin with, this was more or less said as a joke, but then I realized that it was what he had been hoping for, ever since he had come to Europe from his monastery in India—a disciple in the literal Hindu monastic sense, a novice monk who serves his guru and is trained by him like a son, and who will become a swami himself in due course. I was the first eligible candidate to appear. The other members of our group were all elderly or married or both, so they couldn't have become monastics even if they had been ready to.

When I realized what the Swami wanted, I was embarrassed and disconcerted and a bit scared. I think if he had tried to rush me I might even have run out on him. But he didn't, quite the reverse. In fact, he behaved as though the whole decision were beyond his control and mine. 'If the Lord wills,' he was fond of saying. That kind of talk used to disgust me and indeed it still does, when lazy people use it to excuse their laziness. But I had already discovered that the Swami meant it. It was the way he lived. So I started saying to myself, 'Well, let's wait and see if the Lord does will it,' and I stopped resisting the idea or even trying to make myself like it. This was all the easier for me because there I was, living with the Swami anyway, as an unofficial disciple. To take the first monastic vows would simply be making my status official, it wouldn't mean any immediate drastic change, because the Swami fully approved of my going on working for the Red Cross, for the time being. (He was definitely *not* opposed to social work or to any other kind of constructive activity in the world. That's an idea which is always being spread around about the Hindus, that they disdain activity and withdraw from it, and it's a complete libel. They absolutely agree that the world's work has to be done. Only they point out that the *attitude* of the worker toward the work is all-important, and that, in the cultures of the West, this attitude is usually distorted. But I'd better not get started on this subject. I'm supposed to be writing a letter, not a lecture!)

In 1961, the Swami said I could take the first monastic vows—they are called brahmacharya—and I decided to take them. You'll agree that this was hardly a sudden decision, on either side. I had been with him the best part of three years. It's true that this is less than the normal period of probation, which is five, but I suppose he thought he could take the risk of cutting it short, since he had me where he could keep his eye on me, all the time!

The vows themselves are pretty much the same in spirit as the Christian ones—continence in thought, word and deed—only they aren't so much vows as re-solves. I mean, they aren't some kind of trap which you get yourself into, like marriage. No offence! But you know what I mean, marriage as an inhibition which automatically makes possible the concept of adultery.

Even if you do understand why I kept quiet about the Swami to begin with, it may still seem strange to you that I didn't tell you all later. I suppose it is strange, looked at from the outside. I think I wanted to be absolutely sure that I really had committed myself, before I said anything. After all, one may take brahmacharya and still change one's mind about becoming a full-fledged monk. Does that sound very weak and insecure of me? Perhaps it does. But oughtn't one to feel insecure about something as important as this?

Of course I should have realized that you and Penelope would feel cold-shouldered, when I came to England and saw Mother but didn't look you up. Well, why didn't I? The explanation might be, I suppose, that I feared that X-ray eye of yours! It's never much of a problem to sidestep Mother's curiosity, provided you tell her *something*. But I couldn't have fooled *you* by rattling on about my work, and the beauties of Munich and the mountains! One glance at me, and you'd have seen instantly that something mysterious was going on under the surface!

Anyhow, the time kept slipping by and I kept putting off telling you, and then about eighteen months ago the Swami started to get seriously ill. The doctor told us he had four or five things wrong with him—the liver and the kidneys and his heart and blood pressure—he couldn't be expected to last long. The Swami knew this and he took it very calmly. He didn't seem to have any particular regrets about the work in Munich, it was the Lord's will that it was coming to an end. But he did say several times that he was sorry he couldn't return to his monastery in India and be cremated there beside the Ganges. Also, he wished he could have been present when I took sannyas, the final monastic vows. In our Order, it's a rule that sannyas is only given here at the Head Monastery of the Order. I couldn't have taken sannyas without coming to India, even if the Swami had still been alive.

He died in his sleep one afternoon, quite without warning. The doctor had said there was no immediate cause for alarm, and I had gone out to work as usual. That was on October 11th, 1963. When I notified them in India, the Head of the Monastery wrote and suggested I should come out to them anyhow. Then I could bring the Swami's ashes with me, to be committed to the Ganges. And I could live at the Monastery, and we could all get to know each other, and eventually I could take sannyas. The Swami had evidently told them a lot about me already in his letters, so they were more or less prepared to accept me, sight unseen.

After a few doubts and deliberations, I came to the conclusion that this was the right thing for me to do. So I wound up the Swami's affairs, such as they were, and bought a plane ticket out of the money I'd saved from my Red Cross salary, and here I am.

Just before I took off I sent Mother a cable, saying simply that I was leaving for India. As you may imagine, I was less than ever in the mood for explanations at that particular moment, and, as it turned out, I didn't have to tell her any lies. She took it for granted that I was being sent by the Red Cross to work there. My address here hasn't betrayed me, because, as you've seen for yourself, it's just a P.O. box at a local post office at which the Monastery picks up its mail. By keeping my correspondence with Mother down to occasional postcards, on which I've commented on her news without giving any of my own, I think I've avoided arousing her suspicions.

But I'm truly thankful that this period of deceiving you all is over! It was a silly, petty business and I'm not proud of it. I hope this letter has given you enough background material to use on Mother. Just let me recapitulate the main points—

I am well. I am being properly fed. I shall take sannyas soon—toward the end of next month, on January 25th actually—with about twenty of my brother monks. My decision to become a monk is of long standing, made after careful deliberation and *absolutely final*.

I am not and shall never be held incommunicado, as you suggest. This Monastery is not run by Trappists! You ask if I shall ever come to England again. That's a question I can't answer definitely at present. During the next few weeks, that's to say until after I take sannyas, I must deliberately avoid thinking about the future, because it is irrelevant. And when I become a swami of the Order I shall naturally be subject to the decisions of my seniors. Still, I suppose it's on the cards that they might want me to go back to Europe in one capacity or another. So there's no harm in your telling Mother that such a thing is quite possible.

You don't say whether or not Penelope is in Los Angeles with you. No doubt she'll be astonished when she hears what I've done, and amused too. Well, she's entitled to her laugh. Considering my former opinions and behaviour, the joke is certainly on me!

Hoping you are both of you well and happy, and the Children too.

                                        Oliver

My dear old Olly,

       your letter in answer to mine arrived this morning, and I've reread it at least a dozen times already, it fills me with such happiness and relief. Yes, that first letter did sound a little bit like an ultimatum, as you say! But this one sounds like the Olly I used to know, which reassures me enormously. It was so generous of you to take the time and trouble to write me this long intimate account of your conversion (should one call it that?) and of this truly remarkable swami of yours. The picture is getting much clearer to me now, though of course I still have many questions I long to ask you.

       I've already been on the phone to Penny (no, she isn't with me here) and to Mother. Long-distance between Los Angeles and London is perfect, these days, you might as well be talking in the same room, so while I'm out here I always have the feeling I can conjure up Penny at any moment. But the telephone link between London and Chapel Bridge had something very wrong with it when I put through the call to Mother—it sounded like an antique wireless set in a thunderstorm, and I couldn't get them to get me a better line. So, when Mother answered, I only managed to convey to her that I'd heard from you and that you were still in India and in splendid health and very very busy, and that you'd asked me to call and tell her you were thinking of her and give her your love. That was as much as I could get across, in the midst of all the screaming and whistling and growling static. I'm sorry. But I was afraid, if I yelled 'Oliver's a monk!' she'd have understood it as

'Oliver's a drunk!' or something equally misleading and unhelpful. However, I'll get a long letter off to her today, I promise, and I'll try to bring out clearly all the points you want emphasized.

You were wrong about Penelope. She didn't laugh—though I wouldn't swear she wasn't a tiny bit amused, as she is by all of us, most of the time, in her own subtle way. Furthermore, she claimed that the news didn't surprise her in the least. Either she knows you a lot better than I do—from a different angle, *bien entendu*—or else she was showing off her feminine intuition! She sends you her love and says she hopes you'll return to England in due course and instruct her in The Way. She also asks if there's a Hindu order of nuns into which she may aspire to be received, because she wants to renounce the world as soon as the children have grown up. I accused her of simply wanting to renounce *me*, but this she denied hotly!

In your first letter you quite correctly surmised that the business of book publishing doesn't exactly thrive in Los Angeles. I might have ventured to construe this as a hint of curiosity about what I *am* up to here, if you hadn't immediately added that you didn't wish to pry into my affairs—meaning, I took it, that you couldn't care less! This silenced me for the time being. But now the tone of your second letter encourages me to be bolder, so I'll tell you what I'm doing in Los Angeles, anyway. I have a very good reason for wanting to tell you, which will appear in a moment.

I don't know just how well Mother has kept you informed of my doings, in her letters. I doubt anyhow if she herself realizes the extent to which I've been earning the reputation of an *enfant terrible* with our firm. Some years ago, I think while you were still away in Africa, I had my first minor scandal, over the memoirs of a certain Anita Hayden. (You wouldn't have heard of her, but she was one of the leading British musical comedy and film stars of the thirties.) Her memoirs were pretty hot stuff as well as skating thinly over libel, and I, as a very junior partner, had to use all my arts of persuasion to get Uncle Fred and dear old G.B.V. to touch them with a barge-pole. G.B.V. said, referring to Anita, 'give me a good honest Piccadilly tart, any day of the week!' He asked me if I wanted to bring disgrace on a firm whose list had been adorned by the names of some of the noblest (and least-read) Edwardians. However, persuasion won the day, the memoirs were published and they made us such a shamefully large sum of money that the matter was never mentioned again. But that was only the first of my various ventures into vulgarity. I've made some miscalculations of course, not all dirt is pay-dirt. But on the whole I've been so outrageously lucky, up to now, that my elders and betters have become a little superstitious about my luck, in spite of themselves. They warn me tearfully against going too far, they almost wish I'd come a cropper even though they'd have to pay for it, and yet they daren't actually say No to any book I recommend!

Well, this time I have gambled far more drastically than ever before—got myself involved in making a movie! It's to be based on a novel we published before the War—a morally spotless story, I may add, which sold less than five thousand copies. Then, twenty years later, some American writer rediscovered it and recommended it to the film studio he was working for in Hollywood. The studio was interested and got in touch with us about the rights, but lost interest again when they couldn't put together what's called a package-deal. (Forgive me for parading my newly acquired show-biz jargon!) It was at this point that I suddenly became reckless. I canvassed the few people I know who are connected with the films here and finally found two who were ready and able to put a new deal together. They asked me if I wanted to run the show. I said I certainly did. The experience of masquerading as a movie-producer is too much fun to be missed! As for Uncle Fred and G.B.V., they prophesy my ruin and stipulate that not one penny of the firm's money shall be risked— to which I gladly agreed, because we don't need it. However, each has come to me behind the other's back and asked if he might make a small investment in the film out of his own pocket! Which will show you to what an extent I've already corrupted them. I sometimes feel slightly satanic.

Well, now you know why I'm here in Los Angeles—to talk the project over in all its aspects with our American opposite numbers, and then come to a final decision. Now at last I really think we've reached one. We're going ahead with it. During these long weeks of negotiations I have felt severely inhibited because I've had to school myself in discretion, and I was so excited about the whole thing I longed to tell everybody I met. But, until the contracts have actually been signed, we just might possibly have trouble from competitors, if the news leaked out. That, no doubt, is why I've been some-what evasive in my letters to Mother, even—so please don't be so hard on her, poor darling, for her vagueness!

I notice one phrase in your description of the first meeting with your Swami which seems to suggest that you now believe there is no such thing as accident in life—am I right? Well, here's another most dramatic proof of that belief! You see, this projected film of ours (it's to be very spectacular indeed) will have to be shot almost entirely in Malaya and Thailand. As soon as the deal is concluded, I'm planning to fly to Singapore and join our director on a tour of the proposed film loca-tions. And there you are in your Monastery outside Calcutta which, the B.O.A.C. people here tell me, is only four hours' flying time from Singapore, the merest hop, when one's come halfway round the world already! This move of yours, which was apparently taking our paths about as far apart as possible, was actually bringing them closer together again.

You tell me Mother wrote to you hoping I might visit you in India, but I note that you make absolutely no comment on this suggestion, in either of your letters. Is this to be taken as a warning that you wish to be left alone? Probably it is, and probably I should take that warning, but I'm an indecently persistent creature. I don't believe in giving anything up without at least asking for it. So here goes!

Now please be completely frank with me, Oliver, because the very last thing I want is to embarrass or annoy you. My proposal is simply this—couldn't I break my journey in Calcutta on my way to Singapore and stay a few days somewhere near your Monastery, in some inn or hostel? Never mind how dirty or uncomfortable it might be, I'm quite prepared to rough it. I know, of course, that you'll be busy most of the time, especially now that you have this solemn ceremony of sannyas ahead of you. I would most carefully avoid getting underfoot. Believe me, that's one lesson I have learned from that unfortunate visit to you in Africa! I remember with shame how tiresome I must have been, bothering you with questions while you were up to your ears in work with the Quakers. You were so courteous, doing your best to entertain me in your few spare moments, but I must admit I came away feeling that I was the most useless of onlookers and that the best I could do to show my respect for the dedicated lives you were all leading and the help you were giving to those poor sick villagers was to take myself off to the nearest luxury hotel, which was where I belonged!

Even if I could see you for half an hour a day, the

visit would be well worth while, from my point of view. I'm sure it would do me good, just to be within the ambience of your Monastery and breathe in its atmosphere.

Besides, there's Mother. She's so hungry for real news of you. I don't, for Heaven's sake, mean this as any kind of reproach! But if I can tell her that I've actually seen you, and that you're not only well and well-fed (that isn't *all* she cares about, Oliver, and you *know* it isn't!) but also *happy* in your new life, that will support her and keep her going for a long long time. Do you altogether realize how much you mean to her? I can say this now without any resentment. I quite frankly admit to you that for many years I *was* hurt and resentful, because I knew that I meant very little to her indeed. She *lives* for you. And therefore only you have the power to hurt her, which I know of course you'd never dream of doing, intentionally. She's such a spartan person that it's only too easy to assume that she's self-sufficient and impervious, oh, but she isn't, Olly, she most certainly isn't! She minds things terribly. I've seen her minding and not been able to raise a finger to help, or even let her know that I knew.

Perhaps I have no right to talk to you like this, any more? After all, I have no idea what system of values you may have adopted, along with your new philosophy. I've been talking to you as a brother, but it may well be that in becoming a monk you've renounced all such ties. If so, forgive me for presuming. I'll only venture to tell you this—you may renounce your family, but we firmly refuse to renounce *you!*

As for my coming to see you, that's something only you can decide. I promise you, I'll never question your decision. I'll respect it, knowing it will be made by your conscience only, not your emotions. However, I must ask you, please don't just ignore this request. Let me have a word, at least. You don't have to explain, if you'd rather not. Simply write Yes or No.

If the word is Yes, and of course I desperately hope it will be, then there'll be time to discuss details such as accommodation, your own schedule, what rules I must observe during my stay, what kind of clothes will be suitable for me to wear, and so forth. Also, is there anything I can bring you? Books, for instance? And don't I seem to remember that you used to have a weakness for that dark butterscotch which comes wrapped in silver foil (Callard and Bowser)? I notice they stock it in the markets here, too. Or are all such luxuries renounced or forbidden? I certainly don't want to be responsible for a new temptation of St Antony!

Olly, I must say this in conclusion—you can't know how happy and *honoured* I feel that you chose to confide in me as you have. Even if our relationship as brothers no longer means anything to you, I feel you have brought us close together again as human beings, perhaps closer than we've ever been before. I won't harp on this theme because I know how you hate sentiment. I'm afraid I am a shameless sentimentalist, and getting more of one as I get older. (Thirty-eight next birthday, in case you've lost count!) So please make allowances for me. And remember me in your prayers. I need them. *I really mean this.*

With my deep affection,
brother or no brother,
Paddy

Patrick's first letter fooled me completely to begin with, because it worked on my guilty conscience. I was ashamed of my silly childish secretiveness. I wanted him to tell me he understood perfectly what made me behave like that, and then assume the responsibility for putting everything right again, like a true Elder Brother. So I accepted what he wrote at its face value and believed what I wanted to believe.

But this second letter shows the first one up. It's obvious to me now that he was just playing with me, as he always used to. He hasn't changed a bit. And why should he have changed, why should I have expected it? You don't change unless you want to, and it's clear that nothing has happened to make him the least dissatisfied with himself as he is. All the same, quite unreasonably, I can't help feeling furious with him. Furious because I'm humiliated, humiliated because I told him far too much about Swami. I could have explained everything that needed to be explained without going into those things which were strictly between Swami and me. But is that Patrick's fault? Did he ask me to tell him? He didn't even know then that Swami existed.

He's still playing all his old tricks, including that blackmailing sobstuff about Mother. Not that that in itself makes me angry any more, he's so obviously just trying to get a rise out of me. For him, teasing is its own reward. Actually, Mother can't possibly care much about me now. She must be forgetting me already, which is as it should be and as I want it to be. She only needs to keep being reassured that I'm all right, so she can comfortably dismiss me from her mind for longer and longer periods. That's what old ladies are like, and why be sentimental and lie about it? If Mother really cares for anything now I'm sure it's her cats and her grandchildren, in that order.

Even if I could see you for half an hour a day, Patrick says! If he was so desperate to see me, why didn't he ever come over to see me in Munich? No, Brother Patrick is inquisitive, that's all. The idea of this Monastery intrigues him. He'd enjoy coming here and spying around a bit, that's his only motive.

(At this point, I suddenly stopped. I felt, with a strange kind of panic, that I mustn't write another word. At first this feeling seemed justified and right and proper. I took it for the voice of conscience. I said to myself, keeping this diary has helped me so much, through the months I've been out here. It has got me over all kinds of negative moods and aversions. But never before today have I used it as an outlet for personal resentment. Isn't this terribly wrong and dangerous? But then it gradually dawned on me why it *really* was that I was afraid to go on writing. When I wrote that I was humiliated because I'd told Patrick too much about Swami, that wasn't getting down to the truth. The truth is that I'm unspeakably humiliated and shocked to discover that *I*, who am supposed to be spiritually advanced to the level at which I can take sannyas, still feel these primitive spasms of sheer hatred toward my own brother! *That* stabs my ego in the very heart of its vanity. It was already beginning to pose in its swami's robes and admire itself as a budding saint. Now it gets a glimpse of its unchanged unregenerate vicious monkey-face, and it's shocked. It goes into a panic. It tries desperately not to look.

When shall I get it through my head, once and for all, that the ego, the Oliver in me, never will and never can be anything but a vain little monkey? I ought to have learned by this time, after all Swami's teaching and training, to live with this monkey and refuse resolutely to be impressed or shocked by its postures and greeds and rages. Its whole effort is directed toward making me identify myself with it, when I know perfectly well that I ought to be continually dissociating myself from it, calmly and firmly and with complete good humour—if you get angry with it, you identify automatically. That's what self-discipline means. The monkey must be made to face its ugliness again and again. That's why I should

29

keep on with this diary and even write it in more detail than usual throughout these next weeks, being as frank as I can. It's absolutely necessary to bring everything out into the open at last, in the little time I have left before sannyas.)

I haven't let myself realize until now—and at least I'm thankful that I have realized it, even so late—what a terrific problem Patrick still is for me. This is something I have got to cope with, not ignore and avoid any longer. He must come here. There's no getting out of that. I even want him to come.

There was a lie, or at least an evasion, in what I wrote to Patrick. It wasn't because of him that I didn't visit them in England, it was because of Penny. I was afraid to see her then. I didn't trust myself.

And what about nowadays? Suppose Patrick had wanted to bring her here? How would I have felt? I can't possibly tell—because I haven't the smallest idea what Penny is like now. She may have changed so much that it wouldn't mean anything at all if we did meet. That marvellous understanding we used to have together might simply not be there.

Which makes me wonder, how much of our understanding was just in my imagination? What sort of person was she really? Right up to the last moment I refused to believe she would actually go through with it and marry Patrick. Doesn't that in itself prove I didn't really know her? And anyhow, she surely *must* have changed, after living all these years with him.

All right, perhaps I *am* still a bit in love with her. Perhaps I'm rationalizing my jealousy of Patrick by saying he's unworthy of her. Perhaps it's even true that I fell for Penny in the first place partly because she was engaged to Patrick. None of that really matters. It's just psychology, and psychology is merely a sophisticated parlour-game unless you indulge yourself by playing it and giving it the power of truth. I have vowed not to play the game—that's the whole meaning of my life here. In Patrick's world, everybody plays it, and so the precious ego is flattered and cultivated and fattened by being told about its remarkable sicknesses. In our world, the ego is methodically starved to death.

Patrick must come here, and I must face him and our relationship. I must accept him with all his arts and tricks, all the good, all the bad, everything. What's the use of me, if I can't pass this test? What kind of a swami am I going to be?

Enough of this for now. Now write to Patrick. Tell him he can come.

No, better send him a cable. Let's get the machinery started, irrevocably, as soon as possible.

2

Dearest Mother,

as you may imagine, I've been eagerly looking forward to hearing what you'd have to say to the news about Oliver. Your letter didn't reach me until yesterday, when I was in the midst of getting ready to leave, so there was no time to write then. Anyhow, there's really nothing of importance to be added before I can send you my impressions of him at first hand.

I don't wonder you say you find the idea of Oliver in his Monastery 'a little bewildering'! It does sound pretty exotic—a far cry from St Martin's and your beloved Vicar! Olly is indeed a genius at surprises. If we'd been told that he was about to surprise us once again and that we must guess how he'd do it, I don't think we would ever have hit on this, would we? He is among the very few who really have the right to say, 'My thoughts are not your thoughts, neither are your ways my ways.' (Sorry, I don't mean to blaspheme!) But that unpredictability is one of the things we love him for, isn't it?

And isn't it refreshing, in these days of conformity, to know of one human being at least who always seems to do exactly what he wants to do, not what he has to do? I do find that most inspiring—though what would happen to the world if we all followed Oliver's example, I tremble to think! Nearly all of us are the slaves of our obligations, however willingly we may fulfil them. (If you read this letter aloud to Penny over the phone, perhaps you'd better skip that last sentence, or she's sure to take it personally. Aren't I awful?!) Of course, joining a monastery is very definitely an obligation, too, and it's possible that our reckless Olly has got himself caught at last. But I wouldn't be too sure of it. He's capable of breaking out of situations just as drastically as he plunges into them!

Well, now I'm actually on my way to him. We took off from Los Angeles after breakfast, at nine this morning. Or perhaps it was yesterday by now, I don't know if we've crossed the international date line yet. The plane stopped at Honolulu but only briefly, I'm glad to say. There was a violent hot wind blowing, like the draught coming out of a huge hair-drier; such unpleasant clammy heat and harsh glittering sunshine. The airport is very like most other big ones nowadays, with all those ghastly shiny gift-shops. But to prove to you that you really are on the Hawaiian Islands the stewardesses grab you on arrival and throw a great halter of flowers around your neck, as though you were a horse. The flowers must be terribly hot and heavy to carry about, and their smell is sweet enough to make you feel sick, even at a distance. Luckily for me I wasn't an honoured visitor but only a bird of passage, so I was able to avoid getting haltered.

My final memories of California are very agreeable, though. After weeks of having to attend tiresome lunches with executives in film studios and dinner parties at the homes of exceedingly dim stars, it was arranged for me to escape for a few days' holiday. I was motored far up the coast to a district which is still quite wild and unspoilt; cliffs towering sheer out of the sea, seals swimming in the coves below, and magnificent tall dark solemn woods in deep canyons. At the bottom of one canyon, a low tunnel has been cut right through the rock. You come out through it on to a reef which forms a small natural harbour, just enough room for a single boat. The old heavy iron mooring-rings are still there. Perhaps it was used by smugglers, one can easily imagine that it might have been. I kept wishing you could have been with me, with your watercolours. It's just the kind of outrageously romantic spot which really appeals to you!

We shall be in Tokyo by suppertime. India, via Hong Kong, tomorrow evening. I am very well and enormously enjoying this trip. I will write again as soon as I've seen Oliver, of course.

And now remember, Mother darling, you are not to worry about him. I can absolutely promise you, even in advance, that *everything is going to be all right*. I have a feeling about this, and you know my feelings, they're *never* wrong!

Ever lovingly,
Paddy

My darling Penelope,

I'm afraid I have been bad, not writing to you in all this long while. I know how you hate phone calls, and our last few have been more than usually unsatisfactory, haven't they? I kept feeling that I wasn't really getting through to you. No, worse than that, I got an uneasy impression from one or two things you said that you imagined I was behaving strangely—being cold or distant, I don't exactly know what. I avoided asking you about this at the time, for fear I'd only make matters worse, but now tell me, *was* that how you felt? If it was, you had no reason to, *believe me!* You must admit, darling, you do sometimes fancy things. Not that I'm criticizing you for that, it's just one of the penalties you pay for having such an acutely sensitive sweet nature. I love you for minding about my moods, real or imaginary, because that proves you love me. But I can't bear to think of your being even the least tiny bit unhappy, however mistakenly.

I even suspect, and do forgive me if I'm wrong, that you feel my staying on in Los Angeles these last ten days was unnecessary. (I know you were terribly disappointed, as I was, about our missing a Christmas together for the first time, but that was absolutely unavoidable, as I'm sure you realize.) Well, yes, it's true that I could actually have left Los Angeles a little earlier than I did, and made the trip to India the other way around, via England, and spent a few days with you and the Children. That sounds heavenly, as an idea, but just consider, darling, what it would have been like in fact, our being together with the prospect of parting again so soon hanging over us all the time. You know yourself, the few times that's happened, what a strain it was and how wretched, and how it makes a sort of tragedy out of something that isn't in the least tragic— as though you and I were desperate lovers in wartime, counting the last minutes of my leave!

I think that what matters above everything else, when two people have come as close to each other as you and I have, is that we shall always be sensible and realistic. There's always the danger of our getting over-intense and seeing minor annoyances as major problems. Also, when one of us makes a decision, the other must accept it without questioning. Perhaps you'll laugh when you read this and say to yourself, what Paddy means is that *I* must accept *his* decisions! But you know, don't you, Penny, that that isn't so? You know how absolutely I rely on your strength. How I demand from you the faith that holds us two together. You know me, only too well. You know how weak I am. And, don't you see, it's just because I'm the weaker one, because I need you more

35

than you need me, that it's up to me to make this kind of decision—to be sensible and stay on in Los Angeles instead of giving way to my impulse and dashing frantically back to you?

But why am I writing all this? You don't really need reassuring, *do you?*

This letter seems to be all about Los Angeles, but Los Angeles is far behind me now. And my thoughts are far ahead of this slow old plane, hopping to Olly in India, then to Singapore, then on home to you, as quickly as I can manage. I can scarcely believe I'm actually going to see Olly tomorrow night! What will he be like, now? What will be his attitude toward us all? It won't be straightforward and uncomplicated, that much I'm sure of. The first time he wrote to me, I knew at once that he was hinting I should come out there to him, though his pride kept him from asking me outright. But does he *really* want me to come? Never shall I forget that disastrous occasion when he was working with his Quakers in that Congo village and I went down there to see him, very much against my better judgement and at considerable expense, not to mention the hideous discomfort. I hadn't been there twenty-four hours before I began to feel him resenting my presence and willing me to leave at once!

If I seriously thought this new venture would bring him any real peace of mind, I suppose I'd have to be in favour of it. But, alas, all the signs point the other way. In both his letters, as I'm sure you'll agree when you read them, there's such a pitiful admission of insecurity behind his bold determined front. He keeps declaring, directly and indirectly, that nothing, nothing, *nothing* will change his decision to become a monk, until it becomes obvious that he's secretly longing for something or someone to *make* him change it!

Poor dear old Olly, what in the world is going to become of him when he runs out of causes to embrace and prophets to sit at the feet of—feet that invariably prove to be of clay? You never knew Maddox, Oliver's analyst. Olly seemed to regard him as Freud the Father, till one day he broke with him and never uttered his name again. And then there was that terribly aggressive passive resister who led Olly into all that trouble with the police. And at least half a dozen since. Not one of them lasted long. Olly softened them up with his desperate will-to-believe and then mercilessly poked them to pieces with his doubts. Really, you couldn't help feeling sorry for them, he's a demon-disciple! This Swami has certainly lasted by far the longest—his great advantage is that he's dead—but, you mark my words, in the end he'll find himself posthumously seen through and rejected, like the rest.

But of course it's only Oliver himself that one really cares about. In the long run, he's bound to suffer the most from his rejections. Every time he makes one of these breaks, the shock and disillusionment must be greater. So, if there *has* to be a break this time too, then obviously one must do one's best to prepare him for it, try at least to cushion it somewhat. But how, exactly? Well—more of this after I've seen him and found out what kind of a state he's in.

Tell Daphne and Deirdre that I'll send them some little surprises from Tokyo before we leave there tomorrow morning. I'll also try to find something for them in Hong Kong, if our stopover in Kowloon is long enough to give me time to get over there. (Better not tell them that, though, in case I can't manage it.)

Bless you, my darling. Bless you for existing. Bless you for loving me. Kiss the Two Ds from me. Tell them to kiss you from me.

Devotedly,
Paddy

Tom,

   how very strange—this is the first time I've ever
written your name, and it sort of conjures you up! My
heart has started beating faster already and I feel a bit
breathless. Tom. Tom. Tom.

Aren't I an idiot?

I wonder where you are, right at this very moment.
That takes some calculating. Let's see, there's approximately four hours' difference between Los Angeles and
where I am now, over the mid-Pacific. You're four
hours later, so you're about getting ready to have supper. However, the stewardess says we've already crossed
the date line, so we're in Saturday January the ninth.
You're still in Friday the eighth, which means it's still
the same day for you as when we said Goodbye at the
airport. For me, that's supposed to have been yesterday
but it certainly doesn't feel like it! I can remember every
single detail, everything we said and did and everything
I was feeling, exactly as though it were this morning.
Perhaps you weren't aware of the eyebrows raised by
some of the other passengers when you kissed me smack
on the mouth? That's why I made a point of kissing you
right back with equal enthusiasm! But I imagine most of
the people who saw us doing it assumed you were my
younger brother and we were foreigners of some kind,
bidding each other a big Latin-style farewell.

And now you'll soon be sitting down to supper—
thinking about me, I trust. Are you alone? I won't be
selfish and hope you are. I hope you have agreeable
company—well, no, not *too* agreeable! Anyhow, I most
definitely don't want you to be feeling as utterly alone
as I am now. This plane is droning on and on across the
endless ocean. We are chasing the sun, which is big and
dull red, its lower rim seems to have got stuck fast in a
cold blue cloudbank along the horizon. It won't set for

hours yet, because our speed has slowed it down almost to a stop.

The Japanese stewardesses are so cute, half shy and half amused. They bring us drinks, giggling, and they bow to us submissively as if we were mighty he-lords. These seats are too narrow, designed for delicate Asian buttocks. I can feel my neighbour's elbow sticking into me. Wish it was yours!

That coverless and obviously much thumbed-through paperback novel you suddenly pulled out of your pocket and gave me at the airport—*Wow* (as you would say)!! You know, you might at least have warned me what it was about! I suppose I should have guessed, from your wicked grin. Anyhow, I didn't. After we'd taken off, I opened it in all innocence at the first chapter and almost immediately found myself involved in that sizzling love scene between the character called Lance and that younger boy. Did you think that a hard-boiled publisher couldn't be shocked? I began blushing, yes actually! And then I suspected that my neighbour was reading it too, out of the corner of his eye. So I put the book away for private consumption later—behind a locked door!

He's probably reading what I'm writing to you now. But I don't care a damn about that. He doesn't know you, and people who don't know you don't seem quite human to me, at the moment, they belong to another race entirely. In Asia alone there are several billion of them. What a depressing thought!

Oh Tommy, what can I say to you? There's too much to say. And I'm thinking about you so hard, all words seem meaningless. That afternoon down on the reef at Tunnel Cove, with the air full of spray and the shock of the waves making the rock tremble—no, if I talk about that I shall break the magic. It *was* magic, wasn't it,

39

every time we were together, from the first day we met?

When I'm with you I'm a new, quite different person. That's why you must never get upset, Tommy—you did, once or twice, you know—about any of the other people and relationships in my life. They simply cannot touch us, they couldn't if they tried to, because what you and I have together belongs only to us. It doesn't depend on anything else. It exists on its own.

I have never in my life met anyone like you. I only wish it could have happened sooner. I wish—I wish— oh hell! Forgive this drooling.

When shall I see you again? I have all sorts of schemes, as I hinted to you that evening I got so drunk up at your place. I know I oughtn't to have mentioned them until I was sure—in my profession one should have learned the danger of making promises! But I just couldn't keep them to myself. I suppose that was because I was so desperately anxious to hook you somehow! I mean, I'm not naïve enough to imagine that anyone can be satisfied indefinitely by memories, especially if he's young and full of life, like you. I did my best to help you build up a reserve to keep going on. That was why I didn't leave until the last possible moment. But you must have something to look forward to, as well. Otherwise, I'd have no right to ask you to remember me at all. I ought not to be writing to you even.

But now I've been thinking things over carefully— amazing how much thinking you can do on a plane; it's one of the few things they're good for—and I really don't see any reason why I shouldn't get you a job on our film, as some kind of an assistant. I'm sure the work wouldn't be any problem for you, you're so quick at picking things up, and I know you'd get along wonderfully with everybody. It would probably be wiser if you weren't attached to me officially—I don't want to get you talked about, and anyhow I should hate to be in the position of having to boss you around! But I'm certain our director could use you in some capacity. I'll talk to him about this as soon as I see him in Singapore. He's an old friend of mine, and I can rely on him to be discreet and understanding.

That reminds me, be sure to write to me at the hotel in Singapore. (Address above, in case you've lost it.) Of course I would have loved to hear from you while I'm in India, but I don't think it's a good idea. They are probably pretty vague about handling letters at this Monastery. It would be awful if one of yours went astray!

Tom, you remember that evening we drove up into the hills and sat looking out over the lights of the city, and you told me you loved me and asked me if I loved you? We never spoke of it again, but I know you were terribly hurt because I wouldn't say it. I *couldn't* say it, Tommy. I wanted to so much, but I was afraid to. It's such a tremendous word and yet most people throw it around so lightly. I happen to feel differently. I'm almost superstitious about it. But you can be sure of one thing—when the right moment comes to say it, I won't merely say it, I'll shout it!

Meanwhile, there's something I am going to say to you. I know I'm taking a risk, saying it. Perhaps it will make you angry, but I don't really believe it will, because you're so wonderful and generous and you have so much intuitive understanding of me. Well, anyway, here goes—

Tom, I need *your* love, terribly. And I'm asking you *now* to go on loving me, even though I haven't told you I love you or made any promises. Is that outrageous of me? Yes, of course it is. But still I'm asking it, and I don't apologize. I have complete faith in your love, that's my only excuse.

Patrick (not Paddy, he's for the others).

Tomorrow he'll be here.

Went into the Temple extra early, I must have been there three hours at least. In the state I was in, it was impossible to meditate, so I just kept myself mechanically telling my beads. I know that no effort of this kind is ever fruitless, or so they teach you, but this morning it didn't seem to help at all. I tried to offer the whole situation up and say, Your will, not mine. But all the filth out of the past kept backing up on me, like a choked sewer, it was foul beyond words. I felt I could remember every single grudge I've ever harboured against Patrick (I was probably inventing a lot) and I still hated him for all of them. There was such a storm going on inside my head it seemed strange the other people in the Temple couldn't hear it.

So then I went outside and sat for a while on Swami's seat. There was no one about. In any case, they never speak to me nowadays if they see me there. I wonder if Mahanta Maharaj has said anything to them? Or do they just know? The subtlety of their understanding about matters like this still keeps astonishing me.

As always, it helped me, sitting there. I feel calmer now, at least for the moment. But that may be only because I'm so tired.

In the midst of this storm, and all the storms I've been through, I can only try to hold on to three things:

I have known a man who said *he knew* that God exists.

After living with him for five years and watching him closely, watching the way he lived, I'm able to say that I believe (nearly all of the time) that he really did

42

know. I also believe in the possibility of my having the kind of experience which gave him that knowledge.

That man chose me for his disciple. I may be poisoned with hatred and half mad, but nevertheless I'm his disciple. *And he can never desert me.* I have got to believe this, and know that he is with me always, even if I don't feel his presence. As long as he's with me, what can I possibly fear?

I've become more and more convinced during these last months—now it's practically a certainty—that when Swami left his body it was an intentional act. What's more, he wanted me to know it was intentional, in order to strengthen my faith, so he left me various clues, as it were, to convince me in retrospect.

Let me write down the reasons why I believe this:

Swami chose a day on which his health was actually a bit better. His death on that day from 'natural causes' was most unlikely. The doctor confirmed this.

That morning, before I left for work, he seemed more than usually cheerful, playful almost. When I said to him, 'I'll be seeing you at six o'clock, then?' (I made it into a sort of question, I don't know why) he smiled and answered, 'Do you expect me to run away?' And then he added, without becoming at all solemn but in a tone which made it all the more significant, later, 'Don't you know the Guru can never run away from his disciple, not even if he wants to, not in this life, not in any other!' When he said this, I was kneeling beside his bed straightening the bedclothes, and he put his hand on my head, and patted it. He didn't do this very often. I always felt it was a special kind of blessing, because I hadn't asked for it as you do when you prostrate. And now I believe that that also was something done for me to remember afterwards.

Also, when I came home that evening and found him, he was lying in front of the shrine. He had his chadar on over his dressing-gown, and his rosary was looped round his hand. That can only mean that he had deliberately got out of bed and prepared himself to meditate, and that he left the body while in meditation. He didn't just happen to fall dead on that particular spot by accident.

I carried him back to the bed before I called the doctor. I didn't see why anyone else should know. Since I've been out here, I've sometimes thought it was terribly selfish of me, not to have told the rest of our group. It would have helped them, too. I will write and tell them, one day. I suppose I'm waiting until I'm quite sure about all this in my own mind.

Later. The storm is on again, and now I don't feel sure of anything. I feel I don't know what I believe, or why I'm here in this Monastery. Perhaps I have gone mad. Perhaps Swami was somehow deluding himself. Perhaps he is quite dead and doesn't exist anywhere. Perhaps all those millions of people are right, who say that there's no God and that life has no meaning. Why should *they* be the insane ones? They are the majority.

Will things get better when Patrick arrives here? I don't know that either. It's all very well to say that what I'm struggling with isn't Patrick himself, but a monster I've raised up. That may well be true—yes, of course it *is* true. But what's the use of admitting that, if I still can't make the monster disappear?

And if I can't, how can I dare to take sannyas?

3

Dearest Mother,

I sent you a cable from the airport when I arrived here last night. I hope you'll have got it by now.

We didn't get in until shortly before midnight, three hours late, because we were delayed at Kowloon waiting for a plane from Jakarta which then proceeded to load us full of Indonesians, all very small and silent and slightly sinister. There seemed to be dozens and dozens of them, and I had an uneasy feeling that they were being stowed away in the baggage compartment and made to sit on the floor between the seats, and that we should never be able to take off. We were, however, so I suppose they can't have weighed very much! When we finally reached Calcutta, I found to my surprise and delight that Olly was still out at the airport, patiently waiting for me.

Mother, I told you not to worry about him. Now that I can say this with absolute authority, I'll repeat it— Oliver is *well*, and I mean well in every way, mentally and physically. I know you would agree with me, if you could see him. He has lost a little weight, yes, but *not* because of malnutrition or anemia. He has toughened— not that he wasn't a lot tougher than most of us, always—and now he looks lean but very fit. He assures me, and particularly asks me to assure you, that he's getting enough to eat. In accordance with his beliefs he follows a vegetarian diet, but vegetables are plentiful here and, besides, he is supplementing them with vitamins! I know you will be surprised as well as relieved to hear this, it doesn't sound like our Oliver, does it? You remember how, when we were boys, he seemed hardly to know if he had eaten or not. However, the senior monks of this Monastery seem to be looking after him quite anxiously. (Olly was obviously embarrassed when he told me this!) They have an exaggerated idea of the frailty of an English constitution in the Indian climate and are continually warning him not to overdo things and to be most careful what he eats and drinks. Apparently the fact that he has lived in Africa and survived the hardships of the equatorial zone doesn't impress them a bit. They claim superior toxic powers for their own land—a funny kind of patriotism!

Is Oliver happy? Yes, Mother, I sincerely believe that he is. Of course, it's a kind of happiness which could never be entirely understood by you or me. I know—although I'm sure you haven't let him guess it by so much as the faintest hint—that you've grieved because Olly has never found himself a partner in life and never given you grandchildren. (Penny and I have done our best to fill *that* gap, haven't we?) If one has once known everything that a happy marriage and a home can be, then it's hard, I admit, not to feel that happiness *is* marriage and that those who haven't experienced it are simply unlucky. But we mustn't let ourselves be too smug about this, must we? All through history one can find plenty of examples of the other way of life—I don't mean only in the sphere of religion, take Lawrence of Arabia or van Gogh for example— these people who apparently need and prefer to go it alone. I suppose Olly is like that, and perhaps it's what is meant by saying that someone is in God's hands. That

46

phrase always sounds terribly chilly and bleak to me, but it's certainly something one can respect.

It's a descent from the sublime to the prosaic to talk about my own health and welfare, but I know that you in your dear love worry about me too, so I must tell you that I'm far more comfortable here than I ever expected to be, in an extremely clean guest-house which is run by the Monastery and stands just outside its walls. I shall have all my meals prepared for me by a special cook who is a Christian and has been trained to produce authentic British food! In fact, I'm probably better off than I should be in some run-to-seed luxury hotel.

The influence of the Empire is still apparent in this country. The immigration and customs officials at the airport all have distinctly English accents, rather pedantic and Oxonian, despite their sing-song way of talking English. They seemed absolutely without hostility and couldn't have been pleasanter. Still, when one of them stamped my passport and handed it back to me saying 'Welcome to India!' I thought I detected just the smallest hint of proprietorship. It *must* be a satisfaction, after all that has happened here, to be able to welcome the British as mere guests in one's own house!

Of course the friendliness may have been largely due to Oliver's presence. One of them seemed to be on particularly friendly terms with him, and made some remark, evidently a joke, in the native language—to which Oliver answered with apparent fluency. Later I asked him, 'Was that Bengali you were talking?' Olly nodded and grinned—that grin of his hasn't changed since we were boys, and it's all the more charming for being somewhat rare. 'I was practising on him while I was waiting for the plane,' he said, 'I wanted to impress you.' So then I asked him what he'd said to the official and he told me it was 'Yes, I quite agree, that is very true.' So I asked what it was that the official had said to him first, and he roared with laughter and answered, 'I don't know, I didn't understand a word!'

He was wearing a shirt, pullover, flannel trousers and sandals—the sandals were the only Indian part of his costume, in fact. I commented on this, saying that I'd expected him to be 'dressed differently'. As soon as I'd made that remark I was afraid I'd dropped an awful brick, because it sounded as if I'd expected to find him 'gone native'. What I'd actually meant, of course, was that I'd expected he'd be wearing some sort of monastic habit. But he wasn't a bit offended. 'Well I did think of coming out here without changing,' he told me, 'but then I pictured you arriving and this weird-looking oriental running to greet you, and it's your long-lost brother. I was afraid that might be a bit much for you to swallow, right at the start, but I see now I was wrong, you'd have taken it all in your stride, wouldn't you?' I could have hugged him for saying that! I did take hold of his arm and give it a squeeze, but then I dropped it again like a hot potato because I had a sudden qualm that this might be considered as lacking in respect for his cloth or a breach of some taboo. I even muttered 'Sorry!' which was idiotic of me, I realize. But Olly just laughed and said, 'That's all right, I haven't become an Untouchable, you know!' Wasn't that marvellous of him? It relieved me more than I can tell you, because it proved that he hasn't really changed, inside. He hasn't lost his sense of humour. And as long as he keeps that, India can never come between him and us.

Oliver looked in on me this morning, first thing, to make sure that I had everything I needed, and he sat and talked to me while I had my breakfast. Here in the Monastery he naturally wears the light cotton Hindu clothing, like all the other monks. (I've already got some photos of him in this, and I plan to illustrate this whole visit lavishly with my camera, so that you'll be able to have a good idea of how the place looks.) Monks who have taken only their first vows wear white, swamis wear an ochre yellow which is called gerua. (You see, I'm beginning to learn the ropes!) Oliver assures me that Hindu clothes are much more comfortable, more hygienic and better suited to the climate than our European dress. I can easily believe this. Not that I feel any discomfort dressed as I am, because the weather at this time of year is only pleasantly warm.

This afternoon, Olly will come back and conduct me around the Monastery buildings and grounds. It is so dear of him to go to all this trouble, I know he is sparing me as much of his precious time as he possibly can. Also, later today, I am to be presented to some of the senior swamis, including the abbot or head of the Monastery, whose proper title is The Mahanta. (Doesn't that sound awe-inspiring?) As you may imagine, I have a bad case of stage-fright at the prospect of these encounters. For poor dear Oliver's sake, I do hope I shan't commit any faux pas!

Will write you more news very soon.

Ever lovingly,
Paddy

Penelope my darling,

I know that the first question you'll want answered will be, has Oliver changed? Yes, he has, but not in the way I should have expected. I mean, he doesn't seem to have got noticeably older—but then after all, one must remember that he's only thirty-four, even now. As a young man, there was an assurance about him, or shall we say a determination, or even a ruthlessness— no, I've gone too far, I can hear you protesting!—well, anyway, he carried himself very erect and was apt to stick his jaw out, and his movements were purposeful. Now he gives the impression of being far less sure of himself. He stoops towards you when he talks and hunches his shoulders in a funny awkward way, as if he's apologizing for being taller and bigger than you are.

Does he look healthy? No, I'm afraid he doesn't. He is lean and bony-faced and tough, tough enough obviously to take an enormous lot of strain without breaking down. But he's under *great* strain, of that I'm sure, and I doubt if he's getting nearly enough sleep. You can see the fatigue in his eyes. They are bluer than ever and shockingly brilliant and searching, quite desperate. One avoids them, or rather one consciously makes oneself look into them, so as to pretend one hasn't noticed anything wrong.

All these characteristics became much more evident this morning, when I saw him in his monastic outfit, this crumpled shoddy cotton sheeting he has to wear. He is too big and physical for it. It makes him seem rather pathetic, like a hospital patient in a nightgown, deprived of his trousers.

As yet I can't detect any hostility towards me, although Goodness knows I came prepared for it. That may appear later. When he met me at the airport his behavior was nervous to the point of hysteria. But of course he had been waiting for me a long time, my plane was late, he was probably very tired and had no doubt been rehearsing our meeting and winding himself up for it, as I certainly had, so he wasn't his normal self. As he ran towards me he was laughing quite wildly, as I never remember him laughing before, and then he stopped in front of me and stood just looking at me, without even shaking hands. I didn't know how to react to this, so I started walking and he fell into step beside me. Meanwhile he was still laughing or rather simmering with laughter, and his face kept flushing deep red, and he made jokes which all alluded in one way or another to his status as a monk. It was as though he was trying to forestall any possible criticism. Also he was unnaturally polite. He speaks more softly and diffidently than he used to, several times I had to ask him to repeat what he'd said.

There's something almost indecently vulnerable about him. You feel he's utterly exposed. Even the thinnest mask, the one nearly all of us wear for decency, has been stripped off. Do I mean by this that I think he has turned into a saint already? No—but then I don't know what a saint is, so how can I tell? Isn't it just a word we use for anyone who makes us feel acutely uncomfortable?

What I'm wondering is, what on earth do the people in this Monastery think of him? That's one of the many things I'm hoping to find out while I'm here.

You know, Penny, this really is a most formidable country! If you regard it in the aspect of an adversary, it has a kind of passive cunning, something like a judo wrestler who throws you by means of your own weight and strength. Am I making any sense? Probably not, as these are just first incoherent impressions.

I began to get them last night, while Oliver and I were driving back from the airport. We drove through miles and miles and miles of tumble-down suburbs— no, suburbs is too materialistic a word—this was a no-place, dark, featureless, an endless straggling bumpy lane with low unlighted buildings on one side of it and trees on the other, trailing their leaves in a ditch of muddy water. The weirdest thing about this midnight limbo was that it wasn't at all deserted. Dim figures were flitting silently about in wispy smoke-coloured garments; it was as if they'd formed themselves out of the smoke from the glowing charcoal braziers we kept passing. The air was full of acrid charcoal smoke and richly perfumed dust; it's the very breath of this place, so soft and yet so powerful. I felt a kind of nauseating enchantment. How easy it would be to breathe it in and become part of it like its inhabitants, these emanations of dust and smoke! Surely that must happen to anyone who stays here long. That's why I fear for Olly. I suppose that's what I was trying to express when I mentioned judo—Olly's very strength, his terrific energy and manic determination, may actually hasten his defeat. *And isn't this exactly what he wants?*

It was before you and I met, but I know I must have told you how Uncle Fred got a banker friend of his to give Oliver a job in his bank, it was somewhere in the City. Olly actually worked there a whole year, or nearly, and he was so efficient that everyone marvelled. They predicted that he had a brilliant future ahead of him, he was the stuff of which first-rate executives are made, he'd be on the board before he was thirty, and so forth. So what does our Olly do—walks out one day and joins the Quakers! Of course, at the time we all told each other it was merely a phase, he was still very young, only just down from the Varsity. I listened indulgently to his not very tactful declarations that all business is immoral and that banking is the worst, because it's usury, and that those who practise it are the scum of the earth. Bless him, he didn't mean anything personal! Uncle Fred's friend was the calmest and most optimistic of us all—he treated Olly's defection as a sort of mild nervous breakdown, had known lots of similar cases, he said, it was usually the best boys who went through it, in fact it was a mark of real character, and in due course they returned to sanity with an improved sense of proportion, all the better for their little escapade. Indeed, he announced that he was holding Olly's job open for him, being so certain he'd recover. Well, he was mistaken. We all were. Olly had meant what he said, and furthermore, ever since that day, he has proceeded to follow his principles to their logical conclusion. First, business is rejected as evil, then all activity including social service is found to be meaningless, and so you end up with the integrity of doing nothing but contemplate your navel and the fascinatingly frustrating game of trying to know the Unknowable! Believe me, darling, I'm not merely sneering—if I sound bitter it's because this concerns me *passionately*. I hadn't fully realized, until I actually arrived here and saw Olly again, just what a sorry tragedy this is and how near he is to the final curtain of it. Am I going to stand by and watch it fall, without even a protest? No, of course not. I have got to speak out, even if it means losing his trust and affection forever. I must wait for the right opportunity, though.

The Monastery guest-house is bare in the usual cheerless tropical way, but perfectly clean. Oliver warned me not to hang my clothes on some wall-pegs near the window, because thieves have been known to angle with long canes from the alley outside and lift things off the pegs and the nearby table. He told me this with the almost unavoidable pride which the old hand feels in warning a newcomer. Living in a place like this makes you possessive of the discomforts, they're all you've got. I remember how, in Africa, Olly had an air of practically owning the mosquitoes!

(Which reminds me, I had rather dreaded them here, but there don't seem to be many. I have a net over the bed, of course. One slightly spooky thing did happen this morning, though. When I opened my suitcase three or four of them flew out—they'd been inside it all night!)

My food is prepared by a special cook, and it is British to the extreme of caricature. It must have taken generations of memsahibs to train the Bengalis to produce this brassy black tea, this wooden toast, these chalk-white scrambled eggs as dry as leather. I am to eat my meals in a vast bare dining-room at a table which would seat twenty at least. Oliver says that some of the senior swamis will be joining me for lunch and supper soon, but this morning at breakfast I was alone with him. He watched me eat but would take only a cup of tea. I sat in state at the head of the table under a huge propeller fan, like an incarnation of Western capitalism, with Oliver across from me in his Hindu wrapper, representing poverty, chastity and non-attachment. What a pair! How much cruder can symbolism get? I had to fight against laughing, not because I felt happily amused but because I was afraid of hysteria. I know this sounds affected, but it's the truth. The situation seemed funny to me but also ugly, because it was so false, and that's a combination which provokes hysterics. It isn't this new-found religion of Oliver's that I can't take seriously, I know it means something to you and I can at least respect it intellectually. What I can't and *will not* take seriously is Oliver himself as a synthetic Hindu, dressed up in these robes. I'm sorry. Perhaps you'll think I'm being hatefully provincial. Perhaps I am. But I won't apologize for that. It wouldn't be sincere.

During breakfast, I asked Olly a few beginner's questions about the manners and customs here, just so as not to offend him by a lack of curiosity. I longed to probe deeper, into his personal life, but I couldn't trust the tone of my voice, he might have guessed from it what my attitude is. If he realizes this prematurely, I shall have lost whatever tiny chance I may have of bringing him to his senses.

After breakfast, when he said he had to leave me, I went out to explore. There's a lane outside this guest-house, one end of it leads to a gateway which opens into the grounds of the Monastery; in the opposite direction it winds along behind the houses which line the bank of the Ganges. I am to see the Monastery this afternoon with Oliver, and anyhow I wouldn't have dared face it without a chaperone, so I walked the other way. This river-suburb must have been fashionably grand, once— ancient crumbling dark-crimson mansions, the homes of the English and other Europeans no doubt, with nineteenth-century French statues in their gardens, nymphs and classical goddesses, and creepers with great blossoms climbing over everything. Pools full of water-flowers, cows cropping at weeds amidst garbage, walled alleys that wander in and out and stop abruptly, choked with rubble where the walls have collapsed. Mother will absolutely adore the romantic colour-photographs I'm going to take of all this; luckily she won't be able to smell the stink from the open drains and assorted drop-pings! (Incidentally, I've just finished writing to her—I foresee I'm going to have to use up my normal quota of white lies for years to come, reassuring her about the health and happiness of her precious ewe-lamb!)

This morning I was in the wrong mood, I suppose. Under other circumstances I could have discounted the stinks and appreciated the romance, but I can't look at this place except in relation to Oliver, so it fills me with depression and a certain horror, even. Down at the ghats by the river I was watching the men and boys bathing—it's they and their families who are now crammed into the tumble-down mansions, turning them into slum-tenements. They were ducking their heads in the cloudy brown mud-water, then swilling it round in their mouths and spitting it out again. I wanted to yell 'Stop!' It's as shocking as seeing someone take poison. But of course it doesn't poison them, and that in its own way is even more shocking, that such filth should be their daily drink. And they seem so unsubstantial, so humble, so dreadfully *patient*. It's no good, Penny—no doubt we are rooted in the flesh, no doubt we're the most arrogant of spiritual morons, no doubt their traditions did have much to teach us, *once*—but not any longer; tradition is dead when it no longer produces a way of life in the present, and their way of life has failed. When unfortunate innocents like Olly expose themselves to it, it can only corrupt and destroy them.

But I'm getting altogether too worked up! Had better stop here, lie down on my exceedingly hard bed and try to lower my blood-pressure before lunch by reading a good trashy novel. (Luckily I have one here with me.)

My warmest occidental hugs and kisses for you and the Two Ds. Wish me well on my crusade against the Hindus!

Faithfully,
Paddy

P.S. On rereading this letter, it suddenly strikes me that there's one other thing about my meeting with Oliver you'll undoubtedly like to hear. The very first question he asked me when we met was about you (not Mother!); he wanted to know how you were and what you were doing, and he listened eagerly to everything I told him and then questioned me some more. I also took the liberty of inventing a cable you'd sent me just before I left the States, in which you particularly asked me to give him your love. I could see that this pleased him immensely—more than he wanted me to know!

He hasn't really changed. I was right about that. I knew it before we'd even left the airport. But he is *more* everything. He has more assurance. He's slyer. He's more on his guard. Also, he's much more tired. At moments, he looks really dead tired. Perhaps it's slowly wearing him out, this need he feels to be eternally on the alert. But that doesn't mean that he'll ever relax. I doubt if he could, now. It must have become part of his nature.

I'd forgotten how powerfully charming he is. Even when you know all his tricks, he can still charm you. And anyone would have to admit that he looks marvellously young for his age. That black floppy hair with hardly any grey in it, those bright clear eyes with only the tiniest wrinkles showing white against his tan, those firm brown cheeks only slightly too heavy, and those beautiful teeth—they must certainly have had something done to them since I saw them last, they're unnaturally regular. Perhaps one of the dentists in Los Angeles put crowns on them. That's what they do to movie stars, and Patrick is a kind of star, he's fighting middle-age just as they do.

When we met, he seemed almost scared. I think he really is afraid of offending me. That ought to melt my heart, I know, but it doesn't. It only irritates me, I'm sorry to say, because Patrick's way of being scared is in itself a kind of maliciousness. Oh, he treads so softly lest he should step on one of my prejudices, and he jolly well takes care that I shall feel him doing it!

Yesterday morning, I came round early to the guest-house and talked to the cook about Patrick's breakfast, and then I went to Patrick's door to ask him if he was ready to eat. I heard him moving about inside the room, so I knew he was awake. I knocked and called 'Patrick?' and he called back, 'Come in,' so he must have been quite prepared for my entrance, and yet when I walked into the room I found him stark naked. Well, that in itself wasn't surprising. Patrick has never been shy about nakedness; he used to make fun of me because I was. But then he said, 'This won't take a moment, I just want to finish—' and he proceeded to do a lot of push-ups, forty at least, and then about a dozen jumps, raising his arms and landing with his feet apart, then jumping to bring them together again. He did these jumps very deliberately, facing me and grinning at me, with his teeth looking whiter than ever in his flushed brown face. And I couldn't help being aware of his rather big penis slapping against his bare thigh as he jumped. Patrick always had a beautiful body and it is still in perfect shape, he must exercise all the time. You can tell that he's been lying in the sun completely nude. He's dark brown all over, with only the faintest trace to show the part the swimming-trunks have covered.

I was embarrassed and wanted to look away. But Patrick was grinning at me as if he was challenging me to admit that I felt awkward about looking at him, so I had to go on doing it. And I *knew* that he was sort of testing me—to see if I'd risen above the flesh, I suppose, and was so pure I wouldn't even notice if he was naked or not! It would have been ridiculous if it hadn't been rather obscene. God, he is just like a woman, sometimes! It was like some corny scene in an old Russian novel, where the woman tempts the young monk. I wanted to laugh out loud but I couldn't, because I *did* notice and I *was* embarrassed, and that made me angry with him. So I walked away and stood looking out of the window, and needless to say as soon as I did that he stopped exercising at once and put a towel round his waist and went into the bathroom. I told him I'd wait for him in the dining-room. As I shut the door I thought I heard him laugh, but that was probably just my imagination.

In the afternoon, when I went to fetch him to show him around the Monastery, I found him sitting at the table in the dining-room, reading through a letter he'd just written. I offered to arrange for him to have a table in his room to write on, but he said, 'I'd rather work at a big table like this one, where you can spread your papers out—it makes me feel I've got everything under control.' Then he excused himself and went into his bedroom.

Before I'd even had time to resolve not to do it, I'd glanced down at the table. There was one letter already sealed in an envelope, addressed to Mother, and there was the letter Patrick had been reading. All I could see was the bottom of the last page, just a postscript. The rest of it was covered by a sheet of blank paper, which he'd casually slipped over it as I walked in.

Patrick had written a lie to Penelope, saying that, as soon as he and I met, I'd asked for news of her and listened to it 'eagerly.' Also he admitted lying to me, about a cable she was supposed to have sent and actually hadn't, giving me her love. Patrick claimed that this lie had pleased me 'immensely'—'more than I wanted him to know.'

This was so flatly untrue, I could hardly believe my own eyes. Actually, while I was still waiting for Patrick's plane, I'd already made up my mind not on any account to be the first to mention Penny, and not to show any undue enthusiasm when he mentioned her. Patrick could claim he noticed some unnatural reserve in my manner, perhaps, when he talked about her. That's all he could possibly have noticed.

Why did Patrick lie? Was it for Penny? That would mean he believed Penny seriously cared if I'd asked about her or not, which I'm afraid I doubt. Or was it for me? Patrick is anything but a careless person, his very indiscretions are calculated, he doesn't leave things lying about that he wants hidden. I'm nearly sure he meant me to read that postscript—just to tease me, disturb me, keep me puzzled and guessing. So now I must try to forget all about it.

When Patrick came back, he looked quickly at the letters and then up at me, and he smiled a little smile which could have meant anything or nothing. Then he picked up the letter to Penny and put it into an envelope and he asked me if the post office was far from here. I told him No, it was quite near the main gate of the Monastery, and that we could easily go by there and send off his letters, so that then he'd know where it was. I was tempted to add, I expect you'll be using it a lot.

We started out shortly before four o'clock, just as the side gate at the end of the lane was about to be opened to let the public in, after the midday closing. So the lane was quite crowded and I had some private fun observing Patrick's reactions. If only he knew how funny he is! It isn't that he's without humour, he has plenty of it about other people, and I'm sure it's his pride and ultimate support, his *religion*, in fact. It's what saves him, he thinks, from losing his sense of proportion and falling for weird oriental cults—like a certain humourless brother of his who couldn't look on the funny side of things and thus came to a gruesome end, denying All That Makes Life Truly Worthwhile!

Patrick has already created for himself a special way of behaving in India. He created one specially for the Congo too, but that was crude by comparison. Here, he is super-benevolent and super-diplomatic. Watching him yesterday afternoon, I wanted to burst out laughing. Whenever he meets a 'native', he steps aside and pauses just for an instant, it's barely perceptible, as if to indicate that he knows his place, he's a stranger and British into the bargain and he wouldn't dream of intruding, so please ignore him, he should be seen and not heard. When a couple of girls pass and glance at him and giggle together he smiles at them so nicely as if he's agreeing with them, yes, you're absolutely right, I *am* ridiculous, aren't I? Once he met a cow and he stepped aside for her too, and you could almost hear him murmuring deferentially, my salaams, Ma'am, believe me

I'm fully aware of your sanctity, you are Mother India Herself.

Then we got into the Monastery compound and I began showing him around and he asked a lot of questions which were quite intelligent in themselves, only it was like an Englishman who isn't interested in cricket, even, asking an American about the rules of baseball— not about the game itself or the people who play it, but just the *rules*. He was exceedingly polite and tactful, but all the time his eyes had a teasing sparkle in them which meant, be frank, Brother dear, you've had to pretend to swallow this mumbo-jumbo, I quite understand that, but surely you can admit to *me* that you don't believe it any more than I do. I resented this, of course, but not very much; it was no more than I'd expected from him. What I chiefly felt was sheer utter weariness at the thought of even trying to explain to him just what I do believe and what I mean by 'believe', and what's really important to me in Hinduism and what isn't, etc. etc. etc. etc. etc. etc. etc.

He also pinpricked me a couple of times about my 'duties'. 'I'm not keeping you from anything, you're quite sure?' 'I don't want to get you into any trouble with your superiors, you know!'

Showing the Monastery to Patrick brought back to me so many things I'd almost succeeded in putting out of my mind—I've certainly tried to, hard enough—all the negative reactions I had to this place when I first came here. Those crippled children begging outside the Main Gate, those visitors and hangers-on who sit day and night in the Lodge, lounging and gossiping their lives away, the general messiness and casualness of everything, Patrick made me see them again as I saw them then. He never hinted at any criticism, he never even showed distaste at the deformities and the dirt and the bad smells, but I knew what he was feeling and I felt it through him. When we were crossing the small courtyard behind the Temple, one of the brahmacharis was preparing the dye for the gerua robes. The very willingness and cheerful energy with which he was doing the job only demonstrated more plainly what a slow awkward process this is—so much rubbing of the rock against the wet piece of marble produces so little, and the mixture is so greasy and full of lumps. Patrick made no comment, but I felt sure he was thinking exactly what I used to think and finding the same obvious solution to the problem. Soon after I got here, when my brain was still buzzing with schemes to make this Monastery as efficient as a European factory, I had the nerve to go to Swami V. and later to Mahanta Maharaj himself, and tell them, respectfully but firmly, that they really ought to mend their ancient unpractical ways. I pointed out to them that a lot of the gerua dye gets washed out each time you wash the cloth, so that very soon it has to be dyed again. Why, I demanded, couldn't we arrange with a chemical firm to mix us up a large supply of proper fast commercial dye, which would be far easier and quicker to use and would ensure a uniform shade of gerua and would last very much longer? Mahanta Maharaj seemed slightly amused, but he didn't snub me. He asked me gently what would be the point of making this change. I was almost indignant with him for a moment, I felt he couldn't have been listening to what I was telling him. 'Why, Maharaj,' I said, 'obviously—it would save time.' And he looked grave and thoughtful, as if I'd made some deeply philosophical remark, and murmured, 'Ah yes, time—' and then he was silent, and there was nothing more I could say, and nothing was ever done about it.

I'd been wishing all day that I didn't have to take Patrick to meet Mahanta Maharaj. But actually the visit went off quite smoothly, without any particular embarrassment. I dare say I might just as well have been introducing Patrick to some Christian bishop, for all the impression it made on him.

All the time we were in there, I was watching Patrick watching him, studying him for mannerisms, probably, so that when Patrick gets home he'll be able to do one of his imitations. Well, let's suppose that he actually was, what else could you expect him to be doing? What does anyone do, when he doesn't understand something? He fastens on to its surface appearance.

Patrick is the most uncanny mimic I know. Sometimes, when he's talking about someone, he'll start mimicking that person without, I truly believe, being aware that he's doing it. That's the monkeylike side of him. The monkey imitates without understanding. You can't call it sneering—only human beings are capable of sneering. What Patrick does is pathetic, really, because this need of his to mimic shows such an utter lack of contact with life itself. I suppose Patrick has gradually let himself lose this, until now all he can do is imitate its sounds and movements. Poor Patrick—this is one instance in which the word *poor* has a literal meaning, it's what real essential poverty is.

As we were coming down the steps after leaving Mahanta Maharaj's room, Patrick said, in his polite sightseer's tones, 'How charming that fountain is, and that little marble seat among those rose-bushes!' And then I heard myself answering, 'That's where Swami used to sit, in the days when he was living here, before he went to Europe.'

The moment I'd said it I was quite horrified, as if I'd betrayed a most sacred secret. Why do I so often tell Patrick more than I mean to? But that was *all* I told him, and I know my tone of voice can't have given him the least hint that I was telling him anything of importance to me. Perhaps he wasn't even listening. He made no comment, and when I glanced at him next he was looking out across the river.

The first discovery I made about Swami, and I made it only by very slow degrees, was his incredible capacity for concern. Before I could think of myself as truly his disciple, I had to understand and believe that I mattered to him, far more than I'd ever mattered to anyone else I'd known, even to Mother. What makes this kind of concern so tremendously powerful is that it has no ulterior motive, it isn't in the least possessive, and it isn't adulterated with pathos and sentimentality, like most so-called love.

Mahanta Maharaj, Swami V. and Swami A. are capable of this concern too—I'm sure there must be several others, but these are the only ones I can say it about from my personal experience. However, it took me some time to realize that. As I look back on them now, it seems to me that my first few weeks here were even worse than those last weeks in Munich after Swami had left us. I was with the Group then and we could share each other's feelings, also there were lots of practical arrangements which had to be made, and that kept me occupied. When I arrived out here I had the leisure, much too much of it, to indulge in grovelling self-pity and loneliness. Of course I was seldom physically alone, never unless I wanted to be, and the brahmacharis were untiringly loving in their efforts to make me feel one of them, but I couldn't or wouldn't accept their love. I made myself be friendly to them, naturally, but my beastly self-pity kept coming between us, although they may not have been aware of it. Even while I was being friendly, I was on the verge of shedding tears over my sorrow, which I told myself was greater than anything they could ever know!

And oh those days of shuddering dainty-minded

64

distaste I used to feel for everything Indian—their religion most of all! Swami's little Hindu shrine in the Munich flat seemed charming to me even when I first saw it, and probably the very fact that it was an alien object made it better as a focus for one's meditation; there was nothing like it anywhere around. It was a shock to come to this country and see them everywhere, little and big, indoors and outdoors, in homes and temples and beside the roads. What had seemed my private property, almost, was a public possession. I'd grown to enjoy the privacy of having a peculiar form of worship, now it was suddenly invaded by millions of people who'd taken it for granted since their birth!

For a while I couldn't stop being sorry for myself long enough to become aware that Maharaj and the others were watching me. They didn't attempt any consolation. They didn't make light conversation and jokes as they do with outsiders. They even treated me with what I took to be coldness, and how I moped over that! I see now that they were standing aside, so to speak, and letting the spirit of this place take its effect and gradually get through to me at a deeper level.

Then one day Maharaj did a wonderful thing. He took me out of doors as though for a little stroll, and then quite casually he pointed out the seat to me, telling me how Swami used to sit on it every day and how they'd teased him about it, saying that a monk shouldn't form such attachments. While he was talking, Maharaj himself sat down on the seat and he signed to me to sit down too—I suppose he wanted to show me that it was all right for me to. I didn't know at that time that Maharaj hardly ever leaves his room, because of the bone-disease in his hip. It must have hurt him to walk even that short distance, and he probably needed to rest before he could walk back again.

Of course, I didn't immediately realize what it was

that Maharaj had done for me. Obviously he knew that only Swami himself could help me through that bad time and that I needed a focus so that I could feel his presence. Before Maharaj showed me the seat, I had tried sitting beside the river and telling myself that Swami must be present there, because it had received his ashes. But the river keeps flowing and it seems to carry everything away with it, including your concentration. And then, very soon, the seat began to draw me to it. I began going at night or in the early morning to sit there with my beads. A few times I've felt Swami with me there, so strongly that I've shed tears of relief—I'm starting to tremble with excitement as I write this, which is bad, probably. So that's enough for now.

I'm glad I have written all this down, though, because it reassures me. It makes me realize how silly I am to worry about telling Patrick too much. What does it matter what I tell him? How could he possibly understand any of this? He wouldn't even be able to make a funny story out of it. It would embarrass him, I suppose. And then he'd try to forget it as quickly as he could.

4

Tom,

it's late, but I must write this to you before I go to sleep tonight, in fact I know I won't be able to sleep until I've got it off my chest—I have to tell you how dreadfully I miss you.

I expected to, of course, in the way that I miss the few other people I really care about, but this feeling is entirely different. I feel sick, literally. It keeps coming over me in waves of nausea—I'm here and you aren't. Ever since I arrived it's been getting worse, and tonight it's almost unbearable.

You'll probably read this with bewilderment, deciding I must be drunk or crazy. Well, I am certainly not drunk. I doubt if there's a single bottle of whisky within ten miles of where I'm sitting! As for my being crazy, yes, I suppose many people would call it that, people who never felt as I do now and never will because they'd always stop themselves in time before it got out of control. Such people live in perpetual terror of what's inside themselves, they imagine it would destroy them instantly if they were ever to let it out. You and I are different. We can afford to laugh at wretched timid creatures like that and even feel sorry for them, can't we?

To be perfectly frank, despite the acute misery of it, I have to confess that I'm glad I'm able to feel like this—because it does prove there's something in me that's still young and alive and kicking! However, my being glad is my own affair. It doesn't mean I'm going to let you off your share of responsibility for this state I'm in.

Yes, yours, you little devil! Oh, I can just see you making big eyes of innocence, I can just hear you protesting, 'But you wanted it and I wanted it, what's wrong with that, what did you expect anyway, how can I help being me?' Of course you can't help it, Tommy, and I've thanked God you were you from the first day I met you. But that's not the responsibility I'm talking about, and you know damn well it isn't. It's that bloody novel you gave me to read. Well, now I have read it right through, twice, not to mention I don't know how many dippings into some of the sexier scenes. I know you weren't recommending it to me for its literary value and so your feelings won't be hurt when I say that it's probably the greatest trash I ever read in my life—and I'm speaking as a professional reader of trash, remember!—but that doesn't make it any the less exciting. Admittedly I haven't had much experience of this sort of literature. I realize that it's being mass-produced nowadays, especially in your own enlightened country. Funny to think that, when I was your age, even, this book still couldn't have been published openly and sold on the counter!

You certainly must have intended me to get the stunning surprise I did get when I reached that chapter where they go to Tunnel Cove—otherwise you'd have prepared me for it in advance. Of course, I know that hundreds of tourists must have walked through that tunnel and out on to the reef, so it really isn't strange that some writer should have hit on the idea of setting a scene there in a book. But that particular kind of scene and those particular characters! Tom, I've got to know this, *did you deliberately make us re-enact it?* It would be just like you, yes, I can believe it of you, it's exactly the sort of wonderful sweet idiotic crazy thing you *would* do—and *of course* you did it, there's no other possible explanation! You had read the book and it was you who planned the trip and took me there. I love the romantic silliness of your doing it, but at the same time I can't help feeling, to put it mildly, embarrassed! I mean to say, there I was, taking part for all I was worth in a wild scene of passion—it was one of the most insane things I've ever done, if anybody had come through that tunnel we could never possibly have heard him coming until it was too late, with all that noise the waves were making. I was imagining in my innocence that you were as completely carried away as I was. You certainly behaved as if you were. And now I find everything you said and did printed almost word for word and move for move in this damned novel!

Tommy, please don't think I'm angry or hurt about this or that I feel like the victim of a practical joke. Even if you did stage-manage the whole thing, I know that doesn't mean you were just pretending—I'm certain you weren't. You gave me quite satisfactory proofs that you meant what you were doing, on numerous other occasions! And if you got some kind of private erotic kick out of your stage-managing, then all I can say is, I hope you thoroughly enjoyed it.

While I was reading the novel I suddenly remembered something—actually it was on the same night we got back from that trip, we were having dinner, and you told me that there was a character in a book you'd read that you used to think about a lot and hope one day you'd meet someone like him. The way you told me made it clear you meant that now you *had* met the someone, and it was me—which flattered me, of course, and made me very happy. But when I asked you about the book itself you smiled and got all mysterious. Now

I realize that obviously the character was Lance in this novel. With all due respect to him, I must say I hope you consider me an improvement—because the way he talks is a bit overripe for my taste, and I don't greatly care to inherit the author's description of him as 'faun-like'!

Tommy, you are a devil, though! Your not giving me this book until we were separating from each other, what else was that but a really fiendish plan to torment me by continually reminding me of you? It's like those new American capsules to cure colds which keep hitting you every hour on the hour, only this is the opposite of a cure, it makes the fever worse and worse. It brings you here into this room with me, right inside the mosquito-net on this bed where I'm lying naked, it's such a warm night. God, I want you so badly! I want you in my arms. If I close my eyes I can almost imagine —yes, I *can*. . . . Damn, damn, what's the use of playing tricks on myself. If I do that I shall only feel wretcheder and emptier afterwards.

Let's change the subject!

I think this must be the least sexy place in the world. Everything I set eyes on here seems anti-sexual. Take the boys, for instance. A lot of them go around half-naked but they couldn't be less exciting. Not that many of them aren't reasonably cute-looking and they often have good broad shoulders, but the shoulders are so sadly, depressingly thin. And their legs! Wretched sticks, more like birds' legs than humans'. You can't walk on legs like that and move with any physical pride in yourself. And those dhotis they wear—the most repulsive droopy drawers, even *you* couldn't carry them off! From the front they look bad enough, but from behind they're positively indecent, especially if you squat down in them. People squat to pee openly into

70

ditches beside the roads—even very dignified-looking elderly men do this—and then the folds of the dhoti part and you get hideous glimpses of skinny naked shanks. The only well-grown legs I've seen so far were on police-officers, and they were nearly all too fat and enclosed in grotesquely baggy old-fashioned shorts. Oh, this is truly a land where you could learn to hate the flesh! Much as I dislike having to admit it, I'm afraid it's all for the best that you can't be with me here. If you were, you'd stand out amongst all these pitiful under-developed creatures like—I was going to say a sore thumb—no, a gorgeously healthy sexy great big golden Californian thumb! And I'd be dragging you back to this room half a dozen times a day to make love to you, which would be conduct highly unbefitting a guest at a monastery and lacking in respect for my reverend Brother.

Tommy, I know there is going to be a future for us together, there has *got* to be, but I don't want to think about it too much, yet. This job for you in our film could be the first step—I really do think that's going to work out—and no doubt it will lead on to the next step, in one way or another. We must just play everything by ear, as it comes. The really decisive question is, do we deserve each other? If we do, we shall get each other for keeps. That's my firm belief—I can't explain it or justify it, but there it is! Well, it goes without saying that you deserve me, if you want me, because there's no one you don't deserve. You deserve the best, and what the best is, from your point of view, only you can say! Do I deserve you? I would never dare to claim that. But if you say I do, then I'll be the last to contradict you!

I long to see those photographs we took of ourselves with the automatic shutter-release, that morning in the patio when the sun was so hot—you remember, the ones your friend promised to develop. Be sure to let me know how they turned out. Better not send them to Singapore, though, you never know if some officious secretary might not open the envelope! And be a little careful what you write, won't you, for the same reason? Tom, I don't want you to misunderstand this, for heaven's sake, don't think I'm being over-cautious and old-maidish. I know how you hate any sort of pretence and concealment, and I admire you for that. But we must never forget, when we go against the majority, that we're forced to be like guerrillas, our chief weapon is cunning. We can't ever attack openly. That's just exactly what the enemy wants us to do, so he can destroy us. If we're bold and rash, we're simply putting a weapon into his hands. Defiance is a luxury we can't afford.

Of course I honour people who deliberately invite martyrdom and provoke test-cases so that some injustice can be brought out into the open, to make the public begin to ask itself: Is this fair? But a martyr must be prepared to sacrifice the immediate future altogether, and I'm afraid I'm not prepared to do that, because it might mean losing you. I only hope you feel the same way? If you do, then I'm sure when you think this over you'll agree that I'm right, we have to be cunning. There's nothing dishonourable in that, it can even be a lot of fun. We'll play a game against them, Tom, and we'll outfox them and laugh at them while we're doing it. Do you know, I have a feeling that playing this game is going to be what binds us together more than anything else? It'll be you and me against the world! And although we're its enemies, we'll make this idiot of a world accept us and admire us, perhaps reward us, even—that'll be our triumph and private joke!

Oh, Tommy, I feel so much better, suddenly! Writing all this seems to have brought you nearer to me. Now I know I shall be able to sleep—and I'm going to dream about you till morning.

Goodnight,
Patrick

Dearest Mother,

    although I've only been here five days, I'm already getting quite habituated. I can almost go so far as to say that I feel at home—as much at home as someone like me could ever be in a Hindu monastery, or indeed, a monastery of any kind!

In my last letter I think I mentioned the still-lingering influence, here, of the British Raj? You feel its ghost rather wistfully haunting the present, powerless now to exert any direct authority and regarding the scene with the reproachful air of an unwanted adviser. The architecture of the older buildings is full of funny charming evocations of Victorian England. For instance, there's a gateway which leads into the grounds of the Monastery, it's just down the lane from our guest-house. Now the moment I set eyes on this gateway I felt a sort of confused recognition, and after looking it over carefully a couple of times I suddenly realized what it reminded me of—one of the back gates of our college at Cambridge, over which I sometimes had to climb when I returned from trips to London, after hours! This gateway was probably built about the same time and you can detect, beneath the veneer of Indian gods and goddesses, a substructure of good homely nineteenth-century Gothic. What a pity the process wasn't reversed—Cambridge would have been greatly embellished by a few Hindu domes!

At certain hours, the Monastery grounds are open to the public and are treated as a kind of park. This surprised me rather, at first. Of course, some of the people who come there certainly do go into the Temple to worship, but the great majority of them seem just to wander about and sit on the grass under the trees. The grounds are inhabited by numerous white cows. Yesterday I saw one of them approach a group of visitors and get shooed away quite rudely. I haven't been able to discover exactly how sacred cows are, nowadays, and I hesitate to ask Olly, lest this should be a delicate subject!

Beside the main gate there's a small house called the Lodge, which is another Victorian structure in oriental disguise, a kind of cousin to the Gatekeeper's Lodge on a country estate in England. The Lodge seems to be always crowded, even when the grounds are officially closed. Olly tells me that families wait there when they've come to see a relative who's a monk. Also, mail is delivered there—and frequently lost, I should think. And it contains the only telephone in the entire Monastery! The telephone is in the front room, that's to say in the most public part of the building, and you can hear someone shouting into it whenever you walk by outside. No doubt one *has* to shout, because of the noise made by all the people who sit chattering around you!

Everything is delightfully picturesque and all the more so because of certain incongruities. For instance, outside the main gate they sell what look at first like those fat kewpie dolls people buy on piers to decorate the mantelpiece of some villa in Greater London. But, when you examine these more closely, you find they're figures of godlets or holy men! There are also framed photographs which a newcomer from our debased culture would naturally expect to be of American movie stars—only, here, they're of Gandhi and Rabindranath Tagore!

The great charm of the Monastery grounds is that they lie along the edge of the Ganges. The monks in their yellow robes and the women in bright saris make marvellously vivid spots of colour, against the moving background of water. The river at this point is wide and shallow and the tide seems very strong, also there is usually quite a strong breeze. There is an astounding variety of boats. Small steamers with thunderous hooters (one of these wakes me every morning, unless I've already been woken by some tropical bird with an equally powerful whistle!), high-prowed barges which remind you of gondolas, boats with huge square sails like Chinese junks, boats rowed by standing oarsmen which might be galleys straight out of Cleopatra's Egypt. This afternoon I saw two immense haystacks come drifting quickly by in mid-stream, apparently afloat. It was only while they were actually passing that you could see they were on rafts.

Across on the opposite shore there are pink and yellow houses like gaily painted toys, standing among palm trees. Even the occasional factory chimneys aren't offensive, they are so absurdly out of place that they seem merely quaint. And, oh, Mother, you should see that incredible light during the few minutes of tropical evening, just as the sun is going down! It shines through the thin mist that rises off the surface of the river and everything turns golden, a rich old eighteenth-century greenish-gold, exactly like a Guardi.

It's then that you hear the music of the evening service coming from the Temple—very loud, it must be audible all over the neighbourhood—a sort of up-and-down wailing, accompanied by drums and cymbals and stringed instruments, plangent and disturbing, but impressive, certainly. I longed to go into the Temple itself to listen, but Olly didn't suggest it, so I didn't venture to. However, now one of the swamis says he'll take me. He himself admires Bach and he assures me he will quickly convert me to Hindu music!

Three or four of the senior swamis now join me regularly for lunch and supper at the guest-house. Sometimes Oliver comes too, sometimes he doesn't, but I'm certain this doesn't mean he is missing meals and neglecting his health, he obviously has duties which force him to eat earlier or later—into these, of course, I don't pry. The swamis are a very jolly lot, and needless to say I'm able to regard them from a viewpoint greatly different from Oliver's. Oliver very properly approaches them with deep reverence. I'm not expected to and don't, and this makes our relations considerably easier—in fact I might almost claim that I feel I already know them in certain respects better than Olly does! They are very intelligent and very human, and, while they are not in the least hypocritical, they're well able to enjoy the humourous aspect of the solemn role their position in the Order demands that they play.

I told you in my last letter that Olly was going to introduce me to the Mahanta, the head of this Monastery. It was a memorable experience. The Mahanta lives in a little separate house on the river-embankment, built probably by Europeans, for it has a very French-looking fountain in the middle of its garden. The fountain is supported by three stone swans and by two cupids. The swans are all right from a Hindu point of view, because they stand for spiritual discrimination between the Real and the Unreal, but the cupids do seem a bit carnal for these monastic surroundings—however, one of them has lost his head, so is perhaps rendered *hors de combat!* Unfortunately, the fountain has been allowed to fall into disrepair, it doesn't work and its bowl is full of green scum, and the garden is carelessly looked after, if at all. There are rose-bushes, and I suddenly pictured you so clearly, in your shawl and gardening gloves, snipping and pruning! You could restore and transform the whole place within a few months, and, even in its present run-down state, I know how it would appeal to you. You'd love to sit on the stone water-stairs—at the bottom of which discarded leaf-plates and broken earthenware cups are joggled up and down by the river-waves. And of course you would sketch the passing boats.

Which reminds me, near this fountain among the rose-bushes there's a marble seat with scrolled ends, the sort of prop one associates with the less inspired productions of Shakespeare plays—only here in this setting it seems pleasingly unusual. When I remarked on it to Oliver, he told me that it used to be the favourite seat of his particular Swami, the one who was his teacher in Munich and then died. I thought it was really touching that Oliver should have taken the trouble to find out a little detail of this kind, especially one that relates to the Swami's early life in this Monastery, many years before Oliver met him. It proves that our Olly is capable of indulging in sentiment, after all. We used to think of him as the least sentimental of creatures, didn't we? With deep feelings and strong loyalties, yes, but determined not to show them at any price. *I* was the one who always wore my heart on my sleeve!

But to get back to our visit to the Mahanta. His room opens directly on to a verandah which runs right around the house. There were at least a dozen youths and men standing at the doorway, all of them monks. Of course, this living in public is characteristically Asian, and I suppose you get used to it very quickly. When we entered the room itself, there were more monks. They formed a group around an old-fashioned brass bedstead on which the Mahanta was sitting. He is a massive old man, really very big, not particularly fat. His skin is silver-grey in colour and mottled with liver-spots, I don't think he is well at all. He wore a blanket over his shoulders, covering the gerua robe. His feet and crossed legs were partly visible, clothed in long underwear and brown silk socks. I found the underwear somehow disconcerting, yet I hardly know why. Is it that monks are still to us what Victorian ladies used to be—are their undergarments 'unmentionables' which mustn't even be thought about?!

Before our visit, Oliver had very considerately briefed me on the protocol. He told me that I should address the Mahanta as 'Maharaj', which means approximately 'Master' and is a conventional title of respect used in speaking to religious dignitaries in this country. He explained that he himself would have to prostrate before the Mahanta—it's called making a pranam, or taking the dust of a person's feet. (This consists of bowing down and touching the feet of your superior, one after the other, and then touching your own forehead, and it signifies asking for his blessing as well as making a salutation of extreme reverence. Of course, the dust is usually only symbolic dust, since the feet presumably are clean!) I should not be expected to do this, not being a devotee. In fact my attempting to do it—as I easily might have if I hadn't been warned, because in a situation like this you're apt to copy any action, however bizarre, taking it for granted as part of the drill—would have been instantly checked by the Mahanta himself and perhaps even regarded as an offensive bit of crudity. I asked Oliver if I should shake hands with the Mahanta, and he said that that would be perfectly all right, but that it would be even better if I made him a namaskar, a bow with the palms of the hands pressed together as if in prayer. So, having gone through a hasty rehearsal beforehand, that was what I did, and I sensed immediately—I'm usually able to judge such things—that it made a really good impression. Which was good for me and good for Oliver too. He didn't have to feel apologetic for his unbeliever-brother!

Then the Mahanta said to me, 'So you have made this arduous and lengthy journey solely in order to visit your brother? This is indeed a most touching proof of fraternal affection!' That's the way he talks, and it seems perfectly natural, coming from him, because he pronounces his words beautifully and precisely and with genuine relish, as though the entire English language were a classic text from which he loves to quote. The swamis who have meals with me all talk English fluently and more or less like this, but the Mahanta has more style than any of them.

Meanwhile, one of the younger monks stepped forward, took one of the Mahanta's hands in his, and began to massage it. The Mahanta allowed this to happen without the least suggestion of personal involvement, he didn't even glance at the boy, much less express his thanks. In England, this kind of behaviour might have seemed cold and arrogant, here it didn't, because the boy didn't seem involved either. He didn't appear to be doing this *for* the Mahanta, there was no gleam of devotion in his eyes, in fact he seemed unaware that he was handling part of a living organism! Meanwhile, a massive Hindu silence fell upon us all. That too I had been warned about by Oliver, so I prepared myself to sit it out. It's actually very nice and restful to be able to drop all efforts at making conversation and not feel that anybody is being offended.

A few minutes later, some very slight noise made me turn round. Then for the first time I saw what was apparently a whole family, half a dozen adults and as many children of various ages, lined up with their backs to the wall behind me, squatting on the floor. I had missed noticing them as we came into the room, because my eyes had been fixed on the Mahanta. Now I felt embarrassed, because Oliver and I were blocking their view of him. They were evidently there for what's called darshan (again I must ask for your admiration of the way I'm picking up these technical terms!), it means exposing yourself to the spiritual radiations of a holy man, rather like taking a bath under a sun-lamp.

What Oliver had neglected to prepare me for—and he really can't be expected to allow for every emergency—was that he, after he had made his prostration, would normally have sat down cross-legged on the floor as this family was doing. But, before he could do this, a commotion was caused on my behalf, two monks sprang forward simultaneously with chairs for me. As an alien guest I suppose I had to sit high, but I couldn't help feeling that the honour was ambiguous, it might also mean that I was unworthy of the floor! Anyhow, the Mahanta, who is obviously a master of tact as well as spiritual wisdom, promptly motioned to Oliver to take the other chair—thus treating him as my brother rather than as one of his monks. Oliver submitted to this classification with a good grace, though perhaps not with entire satisfaction. . . . I find these nuances of monastic etiquette absolutely fascinating!

Having turned round, I tried to indicate to the family by my expression that I was sorry I was sitting in their light. They didn't react. Probably they hadn't a ghost of a notion what I meant. As for Oliver, he showed no sign of concern. However, the Mahanta did seem to understand, because he caught the attention of one of the senior members of the family and gave him a slight nod, as much as to say, 'That's enough, you're cooked right through,' at which the whole family rose and prostrated before him, one after the other, before leaving the room.

I was watching the Mahanta's face closely as they did this, and I witnessed something very odd, almost uncanny. As each member of the family prostrated, the Mahanta's personality quite visibly switched itself off—that's to say, his face became masklike and his eyes blank, he suddenly wasn't there!

And then a memory came to me—it seemed absurdly irrelevant at first—from my time in the Army, an old sergeant patiently arguing with a prim anarchistically-minded young recruit who didn't see why one man should be made to kowtow to another, as he put it, and the sergeant told him. 'Don't be so daft, lad, it's not the man you're saluting, it's the uniform.' And then I saw, in a flash, that perhaps the same principle was in operation here—perhaps the Mahanta was simply refusing to take these salutations personally and standing aside, as it were, while they were offered to what he represented.

I felt quite proud of this bit of insight and I hoped Olly would be pleased with me for having had it. So, after our visit was over—it ended with some polite small-talk—and we were alone together again, I told him what I thought I'd observed and asked if I was right. He seemed to agree that I was—that's to say, he nodded and grunted. Our dear Oliver, I must tell you, is a little unwilling to discuss the mysteries of his faith with me, or so it appears. Of course, for all I know, any kind of discussion may be officially frowned on here; perhaps you're supposed to believe and not talk about it. In any case, please don't take this as an implied criticism of Olly himself. We must remember that converts are always apt to be more royalist than the King!

I still see quite a lot of him, though not as much as at the very beginning of my stay. As I mentioned above, he has his duties and I assume that these must include some sort of spiritual preparations—meditation, study and so forth—for the taking of his vows of sannyas. The ceremony is to be at the end of next week. So as not to embarrass him by hanging around and seeming to need to be entertained, I've been making excursions into Calcutta. I looked up a man I used to know who's out here on business, and he has introduced me to a few others.

One can't pretend that Calcutta isn't squalid, though the old English quarter, with the palatial government buildings and the open spaces of park and the monuments, has kept a little of its charm. But even this part of the city looks as if all strong colour had been parched out of it by the sun; it's faded to a dirty yellow. And the streets are filthy—you have to be careful not to slip on garbage which has been scattered and smeared over the pavement. Even in daytime the atmosphere is full of smoke from the charcoal pots they burn at night. And the crowds! You get the impression that the houses simply will not contain all these people; thousands of them must be living out of doors. Many of the streets are so full that there's a permanent traffic jam. The traffic ranges from lorries and taxis to bullock carts, rickshaws and funny little closed cabs with louvered shutters. The bullock carts cause most of the obstruction. It's not just that they are naturally slow, they seem perversely determined to be slower. This morning I noticed one little gnome of a driver seated between the huge wheels of his cart and making absolutely no attempt to prod his bullock into action, despite the frantic honking of horns behind him. He merely pointed his stick at its hindquarters, like a magician, a completely incompetent one, pointing his wand!

Mother darling, I'm telling you all this because I know you want to hear everything about Oliver's life and surroundings. If you found out that I'd withheld some detail from you just because it was unpleasant, you'd never trust me again, would you? Everybody who returns from this country is apt to dwell on the horrors of Calcutta, and I'm afraid you may hear descriptions of it which will make you worry about Oliver. What you *must* realize is that everything is very different out here at the Monastery, where it's clean and healthy and one has plenty of space and can breathe the fresh river-air.

I have told Oliver that I'm writing to you and he sends his love. I'm sure his thoughts and prayers are with you constantly. Certainly *my* prayers are no good to anyone, but my loving thoughts are with you as ever.

Your devoted son,
Paddy

Penelope darling,
      high time for another communiqué!

I'm afraid you may have found my last letter a trifle hysterical? I admit that it was written in a mood of mild panic, the mood in which you say to yourself, can I possibly stand this? And of course the answer always is, you can if you must. Already I'm in a state of psychological convalescence, sitting up and taking a keen interest in my surroundings. That doesn't mean that I like them any better!

I do, however, very much like the monks of this monastery—the few I've met, that is. Collectively they are part of the trap into which Olly has fallen, but you can't blame them for that as individuals, and anyhow they are quite adorable. I suppose I'd expected them to be hypocrites or, at best, mock-humble and mealy-mouthed. But now, having got to know them a little, I'm already prepared to believe that they're completely on the level—chiefly because they're so civilized about their beliefs. They seldom refer to them unless you ask a direct question, and there's never the least hint of their wanting to convert you—hypocrites would be much more aggressive and emphatic! They are soft-voiced and playful and gently teasing, but they're far from being mealy-mouthed, especially when the conversation gets on to Red China's ambitions or Pakistan's claims to Kashmir! They never become mystically grave or tiresomely inscrutable. The plump ones chuckle plumply at my jokes, the skinny ones titter. They all seem to enjoy their food and they belch after it. Now and then, one of them exclaims what at first I thought was 'Shiver! Shiver!' but later discovered to be a pious ejaculation, 'Shiva! Shiva!' Being with them is delightfully cosy.

How do they feel about me, I wonder? When I try to put myself in their position, I realize that they must regard Oliver as a tremendous catch. This isn't something I'm imagining—I've seen them looking at him with beaming proprietary pride! And is that so surprising? I don't, of course, know what kind of followers Olly's Swami had found for himself in Munich before Olly came along, but they must have been a pretty stodgy lot of middle-aged transcendentalist krauts. No doubt the Swami's brothers here had already regretfully written off his mission to the barbarians as a flop. And then, at long last, he captures and posthumously presents them with this unique marvellous creature, this his one and only genuine disciple, who has cooked for him, looked after him, abased himself before him in utter devotion, and is an Englishman into the bargain! What a typically Indian victory, a victory without violence! The child of the conquerors is brought, literally and willingly, to his knees! Not only does he embrace the religion of the conquered, he's ready to accept a position of authority, publicly, as one of its ministers—this must actually be, from their point of view, the greatest triumph of all. (However, what I don't think the swamis can possibly understand is that Olly would never, under any circumstances, have become a Christian priest or minister. Most of his fellow-workers on these social projects must have been Christians. Where would have been the thrill for him in going over to *them?* It would have been such a tame sort of conversion. Besides, the Christians believe in action, and that's what he was evidently yearning to give up!)

Now, if the people here think Olly's conversion is such a coup, then they must naturally expect that it'll be headline news in London, read by the English with dismay. (The cream of the joke is that they might not be absolutely wrong, as far as the headlines are concerned. Today, while I was in Calcutta, I ran into an Irish journalist I know slightly; he has been roaming around eastern Asia looking for suitable stories to peddle to the London press. He had heard some exaggerated rumours about Olly and had the cheek to ask *me* of all people if I'd help him get an interview with The White Swami, illustrated no doubt with photos of Olly enrobed and perhaps even communing with a cobra! My first impulse was to kick his backside, but prudence intervened and I tried instead to talk him out of the idea by being very blasé and disowning poor Olly as a boring unnewsworthy crank!)

Anyhow, my point is that the swamis of this Monastery may well have been expecting some sort of counter-attack. I don't mean by the English nation—would Victoria have sent a battleship to bring Olly back?—but perhaps by his family. And what, in fact, does happen? I appear—your official representative, the Elder Brother, that formidable figure whose authority, according to oriental thinking, is equal to that of the Father himself! Are they *really* at all worried by my visit? I very much doubt it. But who can tell? I have no way of guessing what they think me capable of doing, or how well they understand Olly. Not very well, I suspect.

Still, this is a confrontation of a sort. There is some kind of opposition, deep down, between them and me, even if it's no more serious than a game of chess. All right—I'm quite willing to play chess with them, and puzzle them a bit if I can, and see what happens. It should be fun!

How does Oliver take my being here? That's a terribly difficult question to answer. I sense a mixture of hostility—yes, there's that, certainly—and genuine affection. Also I get the impression that he wants desperately to talk to me—I mean, talk really frankly about this whole situation—but that he can't bring himself to, at least not yet. Also, now and then, I'm aware that he's avoiding me. He excuses himself, says he has things to do, but it just isn't convincing. When I ask him about his life here, he takes one of two attitudes—either he's cagey and changes the subject, or else he answers at considerable length, but in a bored clockwork tone of voice, like a guide showing you round a cathedral.

A couple of days ago, I met Olly unexpectedly as he was coming out of the Temple after the evening service. He seemed disconcerted and asked me, quite sharply, what I was doing there. I explained meekly that I'd been standing outside listening to the singing—which, incidentally, I find curiously exciting—no doubt it has its own brand of religious sentimentality, but as a foreigner one mercifully isn't aware of this. While I was speaking, I noticed that Olly was holding something in his hand. He saw I saw it, and made a quick furtive move to slip it into the breast pocket of his shirt. I asked, 'Is that your rosary?' I honestly didn't intend to embarrass him—his nervousness made me nervous too, and I felt I had to say *something*. He looked surly, and said, 'Yes it is, actually.' So then what could I do but ask to see it? He hesitated visibly, for several seconds, before he opened his fist—the rosary was twisted around it. But, as I moved slightly closer to look, he jerked his hand and his whole body backwards, shying away from me, exactly like an animal. I suppose he thought I was going to touch it, which of course I wouldn't have dreamt of doing. Perhaps if I had touched it with my impure worldly hand he'd have had to throw it away! Anyhow, we were both almost equally startled by his reaction, it was so violent and so instinctive. We stared at each other, unable to speak. Then he mumbled that he had to be off somewhere, and he left me abruptly.

This incident didn't discourage me, however, because at least I'd provoked Olly into doing something spontaneous. So I decided to stop being so tactful and prod him a bit harder. (I'm well aware that I'm making myself sound bitchy, not to say malicious, but seriously, Penny, don't you agree that if Oliver is ever to realize what this mess is that he's in, he must be made to drag his new beliefs up out of the murky gooey soup of the subconscious and take a long look at them, consciously and objectively? He must hear how they sound when he has to define them to a non-believer. Perhaps it simply isn't possible to induce him to do this, but that's no reason not to try and go on trying!)

Yesterday I began cross-examining him about his own Swami and his teachings. Olly obviously didn't want to discuss this, but he couldn't very well refuse to, because he'd already told me enough in one of his letters to give me ammunition for my questions. So we went into all this thing about the Red Cross and the Quakers and how the Swami had made him see that the Western concept of social service is fundamentally unsound, because it's based on judgement by results and a belief that social conditions can be permanently improved—which is idiotic, Olly said. This view I find merely asinine. *Of course* conditions can be changed permanently, for better *or* for worse—by blowing up the world, for example! But in all fairness I must admit I realize that that's not exactly what Olly means, and I do glimpse some sort of truth glimmering behind his deplorably sloppy phraseology. It's just that this languid supercilious oriental negativism makes me want to puke!

However, I certainly wasn't going to get myself involved in an argument about semantics, so I just asked Olly mildly what *he* thought the proper approach to social service was. At this, he began to mumble and stumble, muttering that it was very difficult to explain. Again to do Olly justice, we both know that he's no tongue-tied moron, he can be as articulate as the best of us—what he actually meant was that it was difficult, i.e., embarrassing, for him to explain this sort of thing to *me*. However, he finally managed to come out with the statement that the Hindus believe that all one's work should be done symbolically, as though it was some kind of a religious ritual which has no practical usefulness, only intrinsic spiritual significance as an offering to the Supreme Being or whatnot—in other words, what's important is one's attitude to the performance of the action itself, not to its results—success and failure are regarded as equally irrelevant. (Forgive this clumsy exposition of what's probably kindergarten stuff to you; I only include it because it's part of the story.) It was naughty of me, I know, but I couldn't resist such a beautiful opening. I said, in a dreamy faraway murmur, 'To work alone thou hast the right, but never to the fruits thereof'—which startled Olly considerably. 'But that's from the Gita,' he exclaimed, quite indignantly. 'Funny,' I said, all innocence, 'it just popped into my head—you know my unfortunate talent for storing up useless information, I must have heard it quoted by someone, Penny probably.' He didn't like this, I could tell—I suppose because it seemed like poaching on his preserves. 'But, frankly Olly,' I went on, 'I really couldn't care less what somebody wrote thousands of years ago, all that interests me is what *you* think, *now*.' I was honestly trying to pacify him, but my tone must have been wrong, because this only displeased him more. 'You keep saying you're interested,' he said, looking at me very hard. 'I dare say you are, up to a point. You'd better not get too interested, though. It might be risky.' *'Risky?'* I said. 'Why on earth should it be risky?' 'If you really cared what I thought,' he said, 'you'd be forced to ask yourself, sooner or later, if there wasn't some truth in it. And suppose you decided there was, then the question would arise, what you were going to do about it. And that might mean altering your attitude to a whole lot of things. Wouldn't that be a bit inconvenient for you?' He said this with the most aggressive kind of sarcasm, it quite startled me. I felt the situation was getting altogether too serious and tense and that I'd better stop poking him, for the time being. So I laughed and said, 'But surely, Olly, you should be the last person to worry about that. I mean, let's suppose that by some miracle I did change my attitude— whatever you think that is—shouldn't I be, from your point of view, *saved?'*

This made him grin, in spite of himself, and created a noticeable détente, of which I took advantage by asking to see his room. Of course, this was being personal too, in a different way—I'd asked him once before and he'd put me off with some excuse—but now he raised no objection, in fact he seemed positively eager to show it to me. (Looking back on the incident, I suspect he'd decided that the time was ripe to teach me a little lesson. More about that in a moment.)

So he took me over to a building I'd scarcely noticed before, it's behind the Monastery kitchen, right at the back of the grounds, a long way from the river. When we got there, he led me up an outside staircase to a doorway at the top. He didn't invite me to enter, he simply stepped aside to let me look in—and, I must say, I got one of the biggest shocks of my life! (Mother would have rushed straightway to the Mahanta, boiling with indignation, to demand proper accommodation for her boy. She might even have wired our Ambassador in New Delhi! So, in case you talk to her on the phone and she happens to bring this subject up, for Heaven's sake be discreet! Either say I haven't mentioned it in my letters, or, if you're not afraid of having a white lie on your conscience, assure her that Olly has a charming little cell all to himself with a breezy outlook on the river. Which is what I shall have to tell her, anyway, sooner or later.)

What I did actually see was a very large ill-ventilated room which was as bare and stark as a public urinal—the best you could say for it was that it looked adequately clean. It was empty just then, but the entire floor was covered with sleeping-pads and bundles of clothes, and it was crisscrossed by clotheslines hung with mosquito-nets. I imagined myself waking up there at night and wanting to relieve nature and trying desperately to get out of the place in the dark without stepping on someone's face or catching my neck on one of those lines! I fairly gasped with horror! And that pleased Olly, I could tell—it's reassuring to know that he hasn't yet risen above liking to show off a little!

I was so distressed that I found myself cross-examining him exactly as Mother would have. He told me that he has been living in this dungeon ever since he arrived at the Monastery. Yes, they *had* offered him a room to himself, but he'd refused to take it—'For obvious reasons' was his comment, and I'm afraid I in my wicked way couldn't help being reminded of Colonel Lawrence's determination to prove to his Arabs that he was just as tough as they were, and a bit extra! However, Olly did admit that this room was ordinarily less crowded—two weeks ago it was filled up by the arrival of a lot of junior monks from other monasteries of the Order in different parts of India, who have come to take this final vow of sannyas. Olly does have a few more possessions than the others, his European clothes for instance, and these he keeps in a suitcase, somewhere else. But just think of it—no privacy whatever, nowhere to sit down properly in a chair or at a table, nowhere to be even relatively alone except out of doors! (I remembered how I'd once come upon him sitting cross-legged under a tree in the grounds, writing something in a copybook open on his lap—at the time I didn't realize that he had nowhere else to do it!)

Of course, Oliver is used to roughing it, and he has always been unnecessarily strict with himself, but he can't ever have experienced anything as bad as this, before. The way he lived while he was in Africa was luxury by comparison. There were moments in the Army when one felt pretty sorry for oneself, but one always had the consolation of knowing one wasn't stuck there for ever, and at least one was among one's own kind. I must admit, liberal and one-worldly as one tries to be, that I absolutely shudder in my deepest bowels at the thought of spending even a single week shut up all alone with these, well, what else can you call them, *aliens*. No amount of shared belief, religious or otherwise, could make it any better, surely? As a matter of fact, I'm willing to bet that Olly's brother monks shrink back from *him*, in their innermost feelings. That's instinct, and how can you change it?

Seeing that ghastly room made me *really* understand for the first time just what poor desperate heroic crazy Olly has been putting himself through. Now I *know* how awful it must have been for him to come out to this country and find himself in this place, all on his own, without even his Swami to show him the ropes and give him moral support. Imagine the hideous moment when he realized how he'd got himself trapped!

What made him do it? Was it for the thrill of making a complete break? Was it a sense of duty to the Order? Was it loyalty to his Swami's dying wishes? No, Penny, let's be frank, we know our Olly better than that. What forced him to come out here was his *pride*. He had burned his bridges! Where else in the world could he go? To go back to the Red Cross or the Quakers, or anyone else connected with his old life, would have been a retreat, and can you see Olly retreating? He wouldn't *dare!* He'd kill himself first. There's never any way possible for him but forward. In one of his letters he actually alludes to this crisis, in his own inimitable style— says that he went through 'a few doubts and deliberations' about what he should do next, after the Swami had died. A *few* doubts, mind you! Olly is probably our greatest living master of understatement. It would be funny, if it weren't so horribly sad. He must have gone quite literally through *tortures*.

Oh, Penny—*why* couldn't he have come to us, before he made this disastrous decision, and frankly talked the whole thing over? Was it our fault that he couldn't? It must have been, to some extent. We ought to have insisted on seeing him, even though he seemed to be avoiding us. I ought to have gone over to Munich and looked him up, even if it had made him furious with me. If we could have once hammered it into his obstinate head that we loved him and really cared what he did with his life, perhaps this would never have happened.

And now here he is, deliberately preparing himself to take this final step, and here am I standing by, watching him. I suppose it's rather like being with someone who's sentenced to death, with only one week more before his execution. Yes, I know that sounds melodramatic! It does express what half of me feels, but only half. Half of me is desperately concerned about Olly, the other half is hypnotized, as it were, and almost acquiescent—that's the peculiar hypnotic power of this place and its way of life, or rather anti-life. All values are turned upside down, here, and inside out, and it's done with such a matter-of-course air that, sooner or later, one would probably begin accepting them—this monstrously unnatural spectacle of a young Englishman being turned into a Hindu swami would seem perfectly natural and reasonable then! Luckily for me, I'm not staying long enough for the hypnotism to do any permanent damage!

Still, I do have the uncanniest feeling that this situation is drifting out of my hands, that I'm not quite in control of my own actions, even. I feel that the half of me which is concerned about Olly is going *to do something*, intervene in some way, and very soon. Meanwhile the other half of me watches, and is merely curious to see what'll happen!

Don't be alarmed, darling, I'm not developing schizophrenia! I'm sure I'm reacting to this topsy-turvy environment as any normal outsider would. If you were here, you'd understand.

Perhaps it's a tragedy that you're *not* here. Perhaps you could really do something to help poor Olly. But let's not dwell on perhapses!

My dearest love to you all, as always,

Paddy

I almost forgot—I've been on a reckless buying spree in Calcutta. *Saris!* Not the kind of thing you see in the shops. I got shown these privately, through a business contact. They're stunningly beautiful, quite worthy of an ancient maharaja's court—at least, I think so. Hope you'll agree with me! I don't know in what form you and the Two Ds will wear them, but rely as always on your creative genius. Be sure to let me know when they arrive, they're already on their way to you, air freight. Also the things from Tokyo and Hong Kong—but that's not nearly so important.

Am I being unjust to Patrick? That's what I must keep asking myself. Am I even completely wrong about him?

But what do I mean when I say 'wrong'? My attitude towards him is so hopelessly subjective that it's absurd to talk about myself as though I were an impartial observer who could ever be 'wrong' or 'right'. For me, the alternatives aren't to understand him or misunderstand him, but to love him or hate him.

And *of course* I love him—I mean, I'm capable of it. Part of me probably loves him all the time. All of me certainly does, sometimes. When I was going through my Freudian phase, I used to wonder if I wasn't actually in love with him, romantically and even physically. I'm quite sure now that that's not true, at least not any longer. It isn't nearly as simple as that—considering what I've been through lately, I almost wish it were. Now and then I suspect that Patrick thinks it is—when he sort of flirts with me. But I'm afraid the truth is less interesting. Patrick's flirting is just a nervous habit he's got into, he tries it on all ages and both sexes. It doesn't mean anything and I suppose it's usually harmless, except that it has probably fooled a few people and made them unhappy later.

What I do love about Patrick, and always have, is his joy, his boldness in demanding enjoyment for himself and the get-away-with-murder impudence with which he accepts the best as his absolute right. A gloomy old

94

guilt-ridden puritan like me is naturally attracted to a Patrick, however much he may resist the attraction, and in our case, being brothers, we're that much more closely involved. Heredity has made us part of a single circuit, our wires are all connected. At moments I can actually feel and think like him, and that scares me, of course. I get afraid that I'll start behaving like him and lose my own identity altogether—which is pretty funny when you think that my whole life in this Monastery is aimed toward mortifying the sense of ego! To escape behaving like Patrick, I tell myself that his behaviour is evil, and I withdraw hastily into the gloomy self-righteous part of myself, which has nothing in common with him, it's all mine, and I freeze up the connections between us with hate.

Patrick can disturb me so terribly because he can make me question the way I live my life. I'm fairly sure he doesn't do this consciously—he doesn't have to know what he's doing, because he does it by just being himself. And I'm quite sure I could never make him question the way he lives *his!* What I must keep reminding myself is that it's I who give him this power. His power over me is nothing but my own doubt and weakness. If I really believe in what I say I believe in, then a million Patricks won't be able to shake me. I won't feel threatened by him, and so I won't have to cut myself off from him and hate him.

When I write this down, it looks so simple. And in fact on the rare occasions (this is one of them) when I can think about Patrick sanely, I do see how absurd it is to let him upset me. Of all the people on earth, isn't he actually the one who's *least* equipped to judge me? Our likeness and our unlikeness both make it impossible for him to understand what my life is really about. And yet I invite his judgement!

I realize now that I as good as asked him to come

here. If I hadn't subconsciously wanted him to come, I would never have written him the kind of letter I did. I phrased it in a way that was absolutely guaranteed to excite his curiosity—curt, mysterious, with 'keep out' signs all over it. Whenever Patrick sees that sign, he does his level best to nose his way in.

And why didn't I wait to write until after I'd taken sannyas? That would have been the natural thing to do, having waited so long already. No, I wanted him here before sannyas, because I longed for him to reassure me that Swami's teaching is true, and that this Monastery is a good place, and that it's all right for me to become a monk! That sounds fantastic, but it's the truth—at least partly.

And that's what makes me hostile and evasive so often, when Patrick cross-questions me. I'm afraid of giving him unconvincing answers! He notices this, of course, and it only provokes him to tease me with more questions. All these references he makes to my 'duties' —I'm sure he must guess what the situation is. That used to be one of my biggest problems when I first arrived here. I expected to be set tasks and given a daily work schedule, like the other brahmacharis. I can understand now why Mahanta Maharaj treated me differently—duties were the very last thing I needed. Swami must have written him a lot about me, and no doubt even before we met he had a pretty clear picture of my eager-beaver mentality, that desperate conscience-stricken urge to *keep busy*. I used to grumble to myself that Maharaj had given me nothing to do. Then slowly I realized that he'd given me *everything* to do—the obligation to pray and tell your beads and remember God is always there. It can't ever be finished, like scrubbing a floor. Well, I came gradually to accept this other way of life and be deeply contented in it—until now Patrick appears and by his mere presence makes me feel guilty all over again, like a hypocrite who's hanging around and wasting time!

At the moment, I can see how uproariously funny this is. But how shall I feel when next I'm with him? One thing is becoming clear—in order to think about Patrick sanely, I must concentrate on his funny side!

He is a terrific hit with Swami V. and Swami K., and in fact with all the swamis who have meals with him at the guest-house. From their point of view he must be the ideal type of outsider, he knows exactly how to carry on the light table-conversation they enjoy and expect from the non-religious. Oh yes, he charms them right out of the trees—so amusing, so well-informed, so British in the nicest way—and always with that respect-fully hinted undertone: Of course you understand, Reverend Sirs, that I talk like this because I would never dare presume to speak of anything serious to *you*.

The first time I ate with them all together, Patrick told them in his most artless style about this film of his and how he's going on to Singapore to make arrangements for it. And then, with an air of shy confession, he let out that he'd hesitated for a long time before signing the film contract—some mystic instinct warned him to wait, perhaps it was a mistake. 'But when I got your cable,' said Patrick, turning to me, 'I suddenly *knew!* I said to myself, if I go first to the Monastery and see Oliver, then everything I do after that will have a bless-ing on it—so I signed, that same day!' Then Patrick looked round the table, smiling coyly at them all, and he said, 'I'm terribly superstitious, I'm afraid.'

This seemed to me utterly outrageous—I was so ashamed for Patrick that I actually blushed, I didn't know where to look. This time, I thought, he really has gone too far! But not a bit of it—the others all found his story delightful. Swami V. chuckled hugely and said, 'Your motion picture will undoubtedly have a phenomenal success, for you are now under the special protection of Mother Lakshmi, the goddess of good fortune!' Actually, I strongly suspect that Patrick was lying; he just invented this stuff to entertain them. Most probably he'd made up his mind to sign that contract even before he got my first letter.

Being with them at meals embarrasses me unspeakably, I can't help it, and I keep making excuses to stay away. That's bad. These are lies, even when they're only implied—there's no such thing as a white lie, anyway. I must have a genuine reason for not eating at the guesthouse. I've just decided what I'll do—I'll start a partial fast from now until sannyas, just take a little rice and some vegetables once a day. Mahanta Maharaj is always so anxious about my health, but I'm sure he'll give me his permission now, so near the time.

I've been working hard to learn those long Sanskrit mantras which we must all be able to repeat when we take part in the ritual. Swami A. has been teaching them to us, and several of my brother brahmacharis have been helping me rehearse them. They are so sweetly gentle and patient with my slowness. Today our gerua robes were brought to us, folded ready for the great moment when we shall put them on, after stripping off our old clothing in the Temple and prostrating naked before Mahanta Maharaj, to be accepted by him as our new selves, on the night of sannyas. The very youthful-looking brahmachari from Bombay happened to be beside me when our robes were brought. He looked at them in delight and wonder, and then he turned to me with such a brilliant smile of joy and hugged me and said, 'We—together!' I hugged him too, of course, but it was with a tiny conscious effort, and even as I was doing it I felt sadly alien. How can I, with my wretched raw-skinned self-consciousness, ever really be one with these people and the utter simplicity of their feelings?

I can't. Becoming a swami will make no difference. I shall never quite belong to them. I'd better accept that fact now and for the future.

Anyway, this isn't nearly as tragic as I've made it sound. What separates me from them isn't important, not ultimately. What unites us is the one and only thing that really matters.

My darling Penny,

 I gravely fear that this time I have really and truly put my foot in it with Oliver!

I told you in my last letter about this journalist here, Rafferty, who wanted to interview Olly as the British Buddha or what have you. I did attempt to talk him out of it, though I suppose not very energetically—after all, the prospect of those two confronting each other *was* a bit intriguing! Anyhow, my efforts obviously weren't sufficient, because two days ago I met Rafferty on the Monastery grounds. He was perfectly within his rights, of course, the grounds are public during most of the daytime and even an occasional Western tourist sometimes finds his way out here, complete with camera. So there he was, lurking around in the evident hope of catching Olly, which he hadn't managed to do, so far.

Well, I flatter myself that I behaved with considerable presence of mind. I put it to Rafferty that this Monastery is a highly disciplined organization with very strict rules (which was certainly stretching the truth to its limits!) and that he couldn't possibly swoop down on Olly without first getting permission from Olly's superiors. Otherwise, I warned, he might find himself in exceedingly hot water—the Order is large and widely respected and has a lot of influential friends, and the Indian Government takes the dimmest view of foreigners who offend Hindu religious sensibilities, etc. etc. At the same time, I offered to act as Rafferty's intermediary and let him know the result as soon as possible. Naturally I assured him that his chances of getting permission for the interview were good, otherwise I'd have had difficulty in persuading him to leave the grounds. He's as persistent as a terrier and utterly without shame, I suppose such creatures have to be. Anyhow, he agreed to my proposal and took himself off.

That was the point at which I should have gone straight to Oliver, I realize, and told him what had happened. Well, why didn't I? It's true that he's usually pretty hard to find, and I'm embarrassed to go snooping around those awful crammed sleeping-quarters of his. Often, when I do catch sight of him in the middle distance, he's with a group of his fellow monks and I'm afraid of barging in on something top secret. But these are just excuses! To you, in whose orisons all my sins are remembered, I can admit that I was also just vulgarly curious to see what the official reaction to the Rafferty problem would be. Can you seriously call that mischief-making?!

So I went direct to headquarters, that's to say to the Mahanta. After all, it is up to him to decide what Olly may or may not do. Besides, I feel very much at my ease with him, the three or four times I've visited him he has always seemed pleased to see me. And he has another great virtue in this somewhat elusive community, he's always to be found. I don't believe he ever stirs forth from his room!

When I described Rafferty and his project—doing my best to make it sound ridiculous—the Mahanta started to laugh, first quietly and then quite loudly. I congratulated myself on my diplomacy. But I was horribly taken aback when he told one of his attendants to go and fetch Oliver! I felt like a criminal being brought face to face with his victim at the police station.

What made the situation extra disconcerting for me was that when Olly walked into the room I saw that he was almost entirely bald! As it so happened, he had just been to the barber to get his head shaved, this being part of the drill for the ceremony of taking sannyas. They save a small tuft of hair on the top which is cut off, as a symbolic act of renunciation, during the ceremony itself. Actually, after the first moment, the effect wasn't so bad, except for the contrast between Olly's sunburned face and the rather ghastly whiteness of his bare skull—he has a very well-formed head, being shaven shows it to advantage and gives him an astonishingly youthful look.

The Mahanta, who was still shaking slightly with amusement, said to him, 'The fame of your sanctity appears to have spread over the earth, for now one of your own countrymen, a British writer, seeks an interview with you in order that your many disciples in distant lands may read your message to them in the newspaper.'

Oliver looked at me just for a moment very quickly, and I could feel his startled suspicion. He was still puzzled, of course, as to what this was all about. The Mahanta began to explain, but he couldn't remember Rafferty's name and had to appeal to me, which brought me right onto the carpet as the engineer of the plot. There was nothing for me to do but repeat the whole silly story, making it as terse and impersonal as I could —I knew it was hopeless to try to placate Oliver. When I'd finished, there was a short but painful pause. Then Oliver asked, 'Do you want me to do this, Maharaj?' And the Mahanta beamed and chuckled, 'But of course! Why should you not do it?' Oliver said, 'Very well, Maharaj, if Patrick will make the arrangements.' He was deliberately avoiding my eyes. 'Naturally,' I said, 'I'll be glad to do that. What time would be convenient for you, Oliver?' He still wouldn't look at me. 'Whenever Maharaj tells me to,' he said. (Oh, the bitchery of this crushing monastic obedience!) Then he prostrated before the Mahanta and left the room, ignoring me completely.

There was no way out of the situation except to get it over as quickly as possible. I made the appointment with Rafferty and he interviewed Olly yesterday morning. Without asking our permission, he had the nerve to bring half a dozen local Indian journalists and photographers along with him. Poor old Olly! He seems to have been most cooperative—though with an underlying grimness, no doubt—answering all their questions and posing for innumerable pictures. Rafferty was delighted. Of course, the Calcutta papers will be full of this stuff. I can hardly believe that any editor in London will think it worth a real spread. But, supposing it does appear, how will Mother react? With her, you never know. She's equally capable of suing for libel or swelling with maternal pride and showing photos of her bald-headed son to everybody in the village! It entirely depends on whether she decides that the newspaper's attitude to Olly has been what she calls 'properly appreciative' or the reverse!

I have only managed to see Olly once since the interview, and then we weren't alone. I murmured into his ear, 'I hope you don't think this was my doing?' He looked away and answered, almost inaudibly, 'It's not important.' So I judged it better to shut up.

Still I must say frankly that in one way I'm glad all this has happened—because now the situation has been pushed to a crisis, now it seems that we have really *got* to have this thing out between us, whether Olly likes it or not.

If only there was more time! We are getting alarmingly close to Olly's première!

Will keep you posted, blow by blow!

Goodnight, my love,
Paddy

When I first realized what Patrick had done, I had a spasm of rage which was like something you only feel in childhood, I could have killed him, almost.

But then I saw this situation was really offering itself as a test. As a matter of fact, if Patrick hadn't been present, I could easily have talked myself out of having to give the interview, for Maharaj wasn't in the least set on it. It's his own utter lack of interest in publicity—how unlike most European churchmen!—which makes him regard this sort of thing as a quite unimportant harmless joke. And I must learn to take the same attitude. After all, I certainly don't expect to spend the rest of my life hidden away in seclusion from the world. Being what I am, I shall always be an object of curiosity to some people, perhaps quite a lot of people—and even more so if I go back to Europe, which I probably shall sooner or later, for a while at least.

One lesson I learned from the Rafferty incident is that it's very important to enter *willingly* into the game. To submit like a sulky slave, to say you can do what you want with me but I'm determined to remain my uncompromising unattractive self—that's nothing but aggression and negative vanity. No, one must try hard to be pleasant and look one's best, shave carefully, comb one's hair beforehand. (This time I didn't have to worry about my hair, and anyhow they delighted in my bald head, though I suppose I'd have been even more newsworthy naked and smeared with ashes!) Actually I got along quite well with that absurd man and his colleagues. It was embarrassing of course—one would have to be very advanced to do this kind of thing absolutely unself-consciously. One feels a bit of a fake and so one suffers, but that's merely vanity of another sort. It's Oliver who is the fake, and I don't have to identify with him. Next time I shall try to remember that and I hope I shall do better. I'm sure it will come more easily with practice.

Of course it's entirely possible that Patrick got me into this mess without realizing what he was doing. But let's assume that he did realize, that he deliberately arranged the whole thing because he wanted to make me face up to the comic picture of myself which the world will always have—the Englishman in Hindu masquerade, the holy fraud. Even so, I ought to be deeply grateful to him, because this is something I've got to face and it's true that I haven't been facing it properly, up to now. Otherwise I wouldn't have been so furious with Patrick when it happened.

These last three nights he's been coming to the Temple for vespers, with Swami K. It must have been Swami K.'s idea. This can't be anything more than curiosity on Patrick's part. Perhaps he's 'discovered' Hindu Music and decided that it's somehow avantgarde. I find that kind of European aestheticism disgustingly patronizing, but that's only my personal reaction and I have no right to call it a pose, even.

This morning, Patrick did something else which upset me all over again and will go on upsetting me, I know, if I let it.

I was on my way to Swami's seat, meaning to spend some time there with my beads. As I came round the corner of the Mahanta's house, I saw Patrick and Swami K. walking a little way ahead of me. I thought they must be going to visit Mahanta Maharaj, but they walked on, past the steps and the fountain and right over to the seat. I couldn't hear what they were talking about, but no doubt it was only the usual polite chit-chat. Neither of them seemed to lead the way, it just happened. When they got to the seat Patrick did stop, though, as if inviting Swami K. to sit down—which he did, and then Patrick sat down beside him. That was when they both saw me. Swami K. smiled, but he didn't sign to me to come over and join them—not that that in itself proves anything, I admit. Patrick looked slightly guilty, I thought, but that may have been my imagination. Anyhow, I quickly changed my course and went up the steps to Mahanta Maharaj's room, I had something I wanted to ask him, anyhow. When I came out again, about ten minutes later, Swami K. and Patrick had gone.

So, of course, I've been through another violently negative mood. When I saw Patrick sit down on Swami's seat, I felt like some little teen-age novice watching jealously over his guru, his precious property, and snarling at all intruders. Swami's seat is *my* territory. I don't even like to see the senior swamis of the Order sitting on it—and that Patrick, of all people, should *dare!*

But now, that's enough!

I'm beginning to fear that this diary-keeping has been bad and harmful for me, after all. Perhaps I've been deceiving myself about my motives for keeping it. Perhaps, instead of disciplining Oliver, I've been indulging him and giving him power over me. So I'll now make two resolves:

No more entries in this diary, at least not until after sannyas.

I will stay away from Patrick altogether until sannyas is over. Patrick must never meet Oliver again. Next time, Patrick will meet Swami Something-ananda. (I only hope they give me a name which won't be too hard for Mother to pronounce!)

There's the rest of today (about nine hours) and then tomorrow, and the next day, and then it starts. Then Oliver must die.

As the time gets shorter, I run through all sorts of feelings. I'm afraid, and then numb and incredulous; I can't believe it's going to happen to me, *to me;* then I feel quite irresponsible and rather amused, it's a big joke; and then I realize, for a moment or two, that it *is* going to happen, and I'm wildly happy, and then afraid again.

Am I prepared? No, of course I'm not. How could I be? How can you honestly say you're prepared for death? This is a death followed by a rebirth, but for me the death is the important part of it. Swami used to say No, it's what you become that matters, not what you cease to be. But then he was speaking as a swami, from the other side of the experience. I must try in every way I can to make a true death out of this ceremony and leave the old Oliver behind. As for what comes afterwards, I must just have faith.

Tom,

I haven't written for nearly one whole week! It seems incredible when I reckon it up. Now I'm afraid my silence may have worried you. I can't explain it myself. Perhaps it's because I think about you so often and so intensely that I get the feeling we're in communication with each other all the time and actual letter-writing is hardly even necessary. I hope you feel something like that too? Still, I realize our situations aren't the same. You have the right to expect to hear from me. I know I can't expect to hear from you until I leave this place. Naturally I'm longing for that thrilling moment when I walk into the hotel in Singapore and ask at the desk for my mail and shuffle quickly through it, looking for the letters from you! How many will there be— three, four, five, six? No, I mustn't be greedy. How many there are isn't what's really important. I know that a lot of things can keep you from writing often— your job, your classes, people you have to see. I'll be quite content with only one letter, as long as your love is in it.

What I want to tell you tonight is this—as far as I'm concerned, our relationship seems to keep on growing stronger and deeper, although we're apart. I mean this literally! It's very strange, something I have never experienced before with anyone.

Last time I wrote to you I was feeling awful. I needed you so badly. It was chiefly a physical need, I admit, and it was torture, pure and simple. It built up inside me until I could hardly bear it, and then came a terrific release, in a dream. I've had plenty of sexual dreams, of course, but never anything like this one. This was much more than a dream, it was so intense it was a sort of vision. I mean, there was a burning pleasure and then an utter fulfillment with you, nearly as good as that shattering moment we had together at Tunnel Cove. But the whole experience went far beyond just sex, it was actually a glimpse of a life which you and I were living together! That's why I call it a vision. Tom, I'm certain this wasn't an ordinary dream-fantasy built up out of memories of the past. Explain it any way you want, *I know* I was experiencing something which hasn't happened yet and perhaps never will happen, but which *could*. And our act of love, besides being thrilling in itself, expressed what our whole life together could be like—was a sample of it, so to speak. I suppose, as far as that goes, I could equally well have dreamed we were cooking a meal together or hiking in the mountains—

those would have been samples too, and quite as revealing, in their different ways! I wish I could be more specific but I can't, it's all so hard to describe. Well yes, I *can* tell you one thing—this life I got a glimpse of was of such a closeness as I'd never even imagined could exist between two human beings, because it was a life *entirely without fear.*

I've told you how I've always been very much attached to my brother Oliver. I've always felt we could have come far closer to each other than we have, if it hadn't been for his ruthlessly independent, self-sufficient attitude, even as a boy. Oliver is certainly one of the most extraordinary and admirable people I have ever met, but he goes his own way in all things. He doesn't need other people, as I do and as I feel sure you do.

Tommy, since I had that dream, I'm certain that *you* could be my brother—the kind of brother I now know I've been searching for all these years, without ever quite daring to admit to myself what it was that I wanted. I suppose I was frightened off by the taboos which surround the idea of brotherhood in the family sense—oh yes, they encourage you to love your brother, but only as far as the limits they've set—beyond that, it's a deadly sin and a horror. What I want is a life beyond their taboos, in which two men learn to trust each other so completely that there's no fear left and they experience and share everything together in the flesh and in the spirit. I don't believe such closeness is possible between a man and a woman—deep down they are natural enemies—and how many men ever find it together? Only a very few even glimpse the possibility of it, and only a very few out of that few dare to try to find it.

We are going to dare, aren't we? We must, Tom, or we shall never forgive ourselves. I feel as if I haven't begun to live yet, and I never shall begin unless you're ready to stand by me. But of course I know you are. You are marvellously full of courage, it's one of the most lovable things about you.

I feel a bit ashamed of my last letter to you—the part where I wrote that we should have to be crafty and cunning. I see now how cowardly that attitude is. No, we must be absolutely without fear. That's why it's wrong for us to plot little plots, about your working with me on this film, pretending to be nothing more than an employee, and so forth. That's a false approach. It would be an utterly fatal way for us to be together, especially now at the beginning. Everything would be poisoned with lies and playacting.

Somehow or other we must find the time and opportunity to go away, right away from everybody, to a place where we can be alone, until we have broken down all the last little remaining barriers between us— we shall discover what they are by degrees, petty suspicions and shames and pockets of false pride. When those are gone we can face other people without fear and let them see us as we are. We won't be aggressive, but we won't attempt to hide anything. Then it'll be up to the others to decide how they'll react—accept us or reject us. And, do you know, I have faith that we *shall* be accepted, at any rate by the ones we really care about? I believe that our being together is going to find its place and fit in amongst the other relationships of our lives, without even causing any great disturbance! Perhaps you'll laugh at this or get impatient with me, saying to yourself that it's more of Patrick's madly irrational optimism, he takes it for granted that the world must give him anything if he wants it badly enough! Well, I admit to the optimism. But let's wait and see who's right!

I am very glad I came here, Tom. I mean, quite apart from the fascinating experience of seeing Oliver again.

Being in this Monastery and talking to these old men, who are so wise in their own kind of wisdom and so childlike in ours, has taught me a lot and made me able to understand many things more clearly. I suppose I used to be inwardly intimidated by this sort of aloof holiness, so I covered up my feelings of inferiority by making fun of it. Now I shall never have to do that again. I don't mean that I now feel superior because I've lost my respect for these swamis, or seen through them—on the contrary, the better I get to know and understand them, the more I admire them. They can truly be described as holy men. And when I say that they're childlike, I mean nothing bad. It isn't that they've failed to mature. They are grown men who have made a deliberate decision—they want no part of the problems of adult life in our world so they have turned their backs on it. Well, that's their affair. It's true that what they call renunciation is what we would call rejection of responsibility, but nevertheless it isn't an easy thing to do. It even involves sacrifices, very real ones. It isn't easy to turn yourself back into a child again—the Bible points that out somewhere, I seem to recall vaguely.

Children are extraordinarily wise, in their own way. (I have two of my own, remember, so I speak with authority!) You can learn a great deal from them, provided you never forget that they *are* children and that you're an adult. There are many things they just do not know, however, and about those things it's no good, indeed it's plain ridiculous, to ask them for help or advice or even understanding.

I have been talking to some of the swamis about their philosophy and ethics, these last few days, and now I have a pretty fair idea what kind of answers they'd give to some of the more basic questions. For instance, I'm reasonably sure a Hindu monk wouldn't be disgusted, like some prudish Christian parson, at the mere mention of sex between two men. They are far more broad-minded here than we in England or America can ever really be, even if we call ourselves sophisticated, because we've been trained since childhood to regard certain kinds of sex as wicked. To the Hindu monk, all sex is ultimately just sex. However, he'll then tell you that any kind of sex keeps you in bondage to the life of the world, which he persists in regarding as evil! He'll agree, rather grudgingly, that as long as you remain a householder it's all right to use sex for having children—but those who seek enlightenment (and they're the few who aren't merely frittering away their time on earth, from his point of view) must give it up entirely! The plain truth is that these good little swamis have never had sex of any kind themselves and therefore they simply cannot imagine what sex can mean to two people who love each other, and how much more than sex it can become. Since sex is just sex to them, it follows logically that it doesn't really matter who you have it with. I suppose they'd exclaim to me in sheer bewilderment, 'But you've got a wife, so you've got sex already, so what more do you want?'

I hope I don't have to reassure you that I've conducted these inquiries with the greatest discretion and in a most impersonal manner? I'll guarantee nobody here has the faintest suspicion that the problem of you-and-me exists. Not even Oliver. The time may come when he'll have to be told, but not for a long while, and *never* until you agree with me that he should know about us. I'd like it best if we could stand in front of him, hand in hand, and tell him simply, 'We're together!'

Tom, I feel strangely certain that one day I shall have you and you'll have me, somehow, somewhere. Let's have faith that it will happen—*because it must!* As far as I'm concerned, being with you is Life. The alternative is non-living, and I refuse to accept that any longer. You are my one chance. If I miss you, I know in my bones that I'll never get another.

This letter sounds positively mystical, doesn't it? Don't laugh at it, *please*, or at

your Patrick.

6

Last night I broke one of my resolves and this morning I'm breaking the other—I've seen Patrick again, and now I'm going to write about it in this diary. *I have got to.* The only possible alternative would be to tell someone what happened and what we said to each other, and that's out of the question.

Shortly before seven, yesterday evening, a boy came running from the Lodge to tell me I was wanted on the telephone. I was astonished, of course. This was the first time I'd ever been called to the phone since I've been here.

As I trotted across the compound, it occurred to me that the call might well be from Rafferty, and I was glad I had such a long way to trot, because it gave me time to collect myself and get over my petty feeling of annoyance at being disturbed, probably to be asked some more idiotic questions, such as how do I feel about beefeating or do I think we should revive suttee. By the time I reached the Lodge I'd firmly reminded myself that Rafferty and his questions are part of the Divine play of Maya, and was prepared to treat them accordingly.

The Lodge as usual was crowded. Several youths were around the phone, taking it in turns to gossip and joke with the operator. They stepped back to make way for me, but not far, and they stood watching me, talking and laughing amongst themselves. I had to stick a finger in one ear and squash the other against the receiver, so I could hear.

The call wasn't from Rafferty, that much I found out at once. The local operator told me it was from overseas, and to hold on. It must be Mother, I said to myself, and my heart sank. There was a delay while several operators with varied national accents kept coming in and being cut off. Then I heard 'Los Angeles', and I realized that of course it was Patrick they wanted, not me. I don't know why on earth I hadn't suspected this before. I tried to start explaining, but now an American male voice interrupted, telling all the operators to get the hell off the line. It was obvious he was very drunk. He was rather faint and incoherent at first, then suddenly he seemed to burst through, as if he had broken some sonic barrier, he nearly cracked my eardrum, Patrick, oh my God, Patrick, Patrick! So I said, this isn't Patrick, hang on, I'll get him for you. But he didn't understand me. Oh God, Patrick, I'm sorry, I just couldn't bear it any longer, I had to hear your voice, you aren't angry with me are you darling, I love you, I love you! He sounded as if he was sobbing. I yelled, loud enough to be heard around the world (so loud that I actually silenced the background chatter in the Lodge for a moment), this isn't Patrick, I'll get Patrick for you, *wait*, don't go away, *wait*, do you hear me, *wait!* Luckily at this point the American operator cut in, so I was able to explain to her that she had got through to the right name but the wrong brother, and she was to make her party stay on the line because there was going to be a few minutes' delay.

I ran all the way to the guest-house, and found Patrick and Swami V. and several of the others just about to start supper. In fact I had to wait while they intoned the Om Brahmarpanam. When I told Patrick he was wanted on the phone, Swami V. asked, out of consideration for him, if they couldn't leave a message. So then I had to explain that the call was important, it was from overseas—I didn't say where, meaning to be tactful. But Patrick, worried no doubt that this might be some kind of bad news about the family, asked if it was Penelope or Mother. No, I told him, it isn't from England. Where's it from then, he asked. I told him, Los Angeles. He looked startled, but only for an instant. Then he said casually, oh yes of course, it must be something about our film, and he excused himself to the swamis and we went out of the room together.

As soon as we were outside, Patrick asked me, it *was* from the film people, wasn't it? No, I said. He turned and stared at me, How do you know it wasn't he asked. Because I talked to him whoever it was, I said, and I think you'd better hurry, he seems pretty upset. Then I saw Patrick was really worried. He didn't ask me any more; he started to run. We ran together down the lane, but when we got to the gate we found it was locked! They must have locked it while I was in the guest-house. This was just about the time they're supposed to, but I hadn't thought of that, anyhow they almost never do it punctually. I knew one or other of the swamis would have a key to the gate with him, and the cook has one, in case of emergencies. I was going to tell Patrick this and then run back to the guest-house for it. But without the slightest hesitation, before I could say anything, he scrambled up the wall. At the top he paused for a moment and looked down at me and grinned. (I remember thinking that that grin was of the very essence of Patrick—although he was obviously disturbed about this mysterious phone call, he could forget it entirely to enjoy the fun and triumph of having climbed the wall!) Then he turned and jumped down on the other side.

As for me, I'd already followed him, instinctively

almost, just as Little Brother used to follow Big Brother in the days of our childhood. In fact, I was on top of the wall before he'd even had time to recover his balance from his jump to the ground. But then I realized that he naturally wouldn't want me there while he was telephoning. So I stayed perched up on the wall, feeling a bit silly. Patrick ran off towards the Lodge without looking back. After a moment I jumped down on the outside of the wall and walked back to the guest-house to get a key, so that Patrick would find the gate open for him on his return.

It was only then, actually, that I remembered my resolve not to see Patrick again until after sannyas. I decided to make myself scarce as soon as I'd brought the key back. I knew that this was what I ought to do and I really meant to do it—although of course I was horribly curious about Patrick's drunken caller.

However, when I got to the guest-house, Swami A. took the matter out of my hands by saying that he wanted to talk to me. But first he and Swami V. insisted on my eating a few spoonfuls of rice and dal, joking about my great austerities and how thin I looked. I felt the love in their jokes very strongly, more than I ever have before.

And then Patrick returned. I could see that he was upset, although he tried to hide it. Also, rather to my surprise, he seemed genuinely glad to find me still there —I'd expected that he might feel embarrassed, knowing what I knew about the call. He sat down to have his supper, making an obvious effort to appear at ease. Then Swami A. asked me to come outside with him on to the porch. As we went out, Patrick said to me, can I see you later? That really put me on the spot, because I could only have got out of it by telling him some direct lie about my duties, right in the presence of the swamis. So I had to say yes. When Swami A. and I were outside, he gave me some additional instructions and explanations about the shraddha ceremony. Meanwhile, Patrick finished eating. He came out of the house with the other swamis and we all walked along the lane to the gate, where we said goodnight to them.

When they'd gone Patrick said, I feel like walking around for a bit, is that all right with you? So we went into the grounds and down to the river-bank and began walking back and forth along it, between the bathing-ghat and the Monastery wall. Although it was still relatively early, there was no one about. It always seems a little strange to me, on the rare occasions when it happens, to be absolutely alone with another person, in this overcrowded country. It was a dark night, heavy and cloudy and warm. You could faintly smell charcoal smoke drifting up the river from the city; I rather like the smell when it isn't too strong. The water was just dimly visible, with half a dozen weak yellow lights dotted over it, on boats.

For quite a long while we walked in silence. Then Patrick said, in an unnaturally solemn tone of voice, Oliver, I'm going to forget that you're my brother, I want to talk to you like people do to a priest. (Although Patrick's tone was utterly unconvincing and obviously part of an act, I have to admit that this was a psychologically clever opening. With his unerring instinct for flattery, he was turning me into a swami already and himself into my first disciple!) And then he even added to the flattery by saying with a chuckle, not that I'd be caught dead telling a priest what I'm going to tell you! I had to laugh too, partly at Patrick and partly at myself, for letting him seduce me into joining him in this absurd playacting.

I don't know how much he said to you on that phone, Patrick said, or how much you've guessed, but that makes no difference, because I realize now I've got to tell you the whole thing, anyway.

When he said that, I felt a sudden misgiving. In spite of my curiosity I had an inkling I might be sorry later that I'd heard what I was about to hear. Are you sure you want to tell me this, I asked him, I mean is it really necessary? But Patrick said, I've never been surer of anything, I *need* to know that you know this about me. So then I couldn't make any further objection. Patrick asked me not to say anything until he'd finished, and I promised I wouldn't.

Then he launched into an immensely long account of how he'd met this young American named Tom in Los Angeles and how they'd started having a love-affair with each other. I say it was immensely long because I kept becoming aware again and again that he was spinning it out far more than was necessary. I don't mean that I was bored for one moment, I was fascinated, almost painfully so. Patrick described every single meeting between them—beginning with some bar into which Patrick had ventured because he guessed what kind of place it was and couldn't resist, although he was afraid. It was there that he first saw Tom and talked to him. After that they used to meet either at Tom's flat or at out-of-the-way restaurants, because Patrick didn't dare bring Tom to his own hotel and was constantly anxious lest they should run into one or other of his business friends—Tom, I gathered, was apt to behave in a compromising manner, when they were together in public.

Taking refuge in my role of father-confessor, I tried to listen as objectively as I could to what he was telling me, reminding myself sternly that this was just another sample of Maya, just one of the many forms of our bondage to illusion, etc., etc. But I couldn't succeed in being objective for more than a few seconds at a time.

It wasn't that I was shocked, at least not for the conventional reasons. It wasn't even that I was much surprised. I suppose I've always known and accepted this about Patrick—and what do I mean by 'this', anyway? I sound just like a Christian, filing him under B for bisexuality (with a cross-reference to A for adultery) in the sin-catalogue. No, what I mean is that I've always known Patrick wouldn't respect the accepted ground-rules. You can't possibly tell someone like him that he mustn't do that and he may do this but only subject to the following restrictions and exceptions—that's not his nature.

If I *was* shocked, it wasn't by Patrick's story, but by the way he told it. When he started off, his language was very restrained, in fact it was sometimes almost comically formal. He used expressions like, 'I told Tom that my attraction to him wasn't Platonic' and 'that was the night we actually became intimate.' But soon his tone changed and he began talking very frankly and using four-letter words with a sort of aggressive relish. For instance, he told me how Tom and he had driven to some deserted cove up the coast to the north for a weekend, and how they'd been on a rock right above the sea and Tom had grabbed hold of him and they had torn off each other's clothes. I suppose it was really a relatively ordinary scene of lust, but Patrick made it sound strangely horrible, uncanny and bestial, like two animals devouring each other alive. He described exactly what they did to each other, and I noticed once again how fetishistic the words can be that we use for sexual acts. It was as if the mere uttering of them was nearly as exciting to Patrick as the act itself.

At least, that was what I thought at first—that he was getting a personal thrill, a sexual kick, out of talking like this. But then I got the suspicion, and it grew into a certainty, that he was trying to excite me, not himself! When I realized this, it seemed terribly silly of him and at the same time somehow sinister—and I was shocked, though less shocked than puzzled. Why was he doing it? Out of sheer mischief? Was it the same as when he paraded naked in front of me, that first morning? No, this was different and, as I say, sinister, because after all this is a serious relationship he has got himself into. Whatever kind of a person this boy Tom may be, it's obvious that he really does care about Patrick a great deal and his feelings aren't something to be sneered or laughed at. I didn't like the way Patrick talked about what had just happened—poor Tom working himself up into such a misery of loneliness that he'd sat up drinking all night and made this desperate hysterical phone call. (Patrick calculated that it must have been after five o'clock in the morning in Los Angeles when Tom finally got put through to us here.) Patrick affected to find the whole thing rather amusing, but I'm sure that was a cover-up. I'm sure that Tom's call has angered and upset Patrick far more than he'll admit. I could tell this all the more easily because I couldn't see his face in the darkness. I had to concentrate entirely on his voice, and it gave him away.

When he had finished at last there was a very long pause. As a matter of fact I had made up my mind not to speak first, because I wanted to force Patrick out into the open, as it were. I could almost feel him willing me to speak and then becoming irritated because I maintained my silence.

So at length he asked, quite irritably, well, aren't you going to say *anything?* What do you expect me to say, I said. And I honestly meant that, I wondered just what he did expect. I see, said Patrick sarcastically, a spokesman for the Celestial Embassy declines absolutely to comment on the situation. There didn't seem to be an answer to this, so I kept quiet. Or are you too shocked to speak, Patrick asked. Of course not, I said, but I've told you once already, I don't know what I'm supposed to say. Really, Oliver, said Patrick, one doesn't envy your unfortunate disciples when they start coming to you for guidance. It'll be a case of the hungry sheep look up and are not fed. In the first place, I told him, becoming a swami doesn't necessarily mean that you ever have any disciples. Accepting disciples is regarded as a very serious responsibility. Only a few of the senior monks of our Order have them. And in the second place, I don't know why you're talking about guidance. You're surely not asking me for that, are you, or even ordinary advice?

Patrick didn't answer this directly. Do you think I'm awfully wicked, Olly? Do you think I'm damned? I know you don't believe in damnation in the same sense the Christians do. But there must be *somewhere* one can get oneself sent to—Hell-with-a-time-limit, what? I laughed out loud. No, seriously, said Patrick, I'm not trying to be funny. Suppose you were a doctor and I had cancer, you'd tell me, wouldn't you? I might or I might not, I said. Anyhow it's a completely false analogy. What do I know about damnation?

You know damn well what you think. (How characteristic of Patrick that was, that little play on the word! And his manner, half aggressively challenging, half making fun of itself. Yes, he was serious in his own particular way, and yet at the same time he wasn't.) Very well, Oliver, if you refuse to tell me what you think, I'll do it for you—you think I'm unfit to go on living with Penny and our children.

Patrick, I said, if that's a specimen of how you think I think, it means you must regard me as a hopeless puritanical ass. Well, perhaps I am one. But, if I am, why ask for my opinion? You know your own problems from the inside. What can a puritan tell you about them? Puritans can't possibly understand things like this.

Sorry (I could tell from Patrick's tone that he was grinning) no offence intended. *I'd* certainly never dream of calling you a puritan, if that means someone who's frigid and can't understand emotion. And don't *you* underestimate yourself, Olly—you're capable of generating more emotion than all the rest of us put together, as you must know even better than I do. Or do you dislike admitting that, nowadays?

I was stung, of course, but I didn't retort—so Patrick continued with his prodding. Granted that you aren't shocked and aren't a puritan, he said, you still must have *some* sort of reaction to what I've told you, surely? I mean to say, here's a problem or a dilemma or a plain old bloody mess, whatever you want to call it—here are three human beings involved and you know two of them exceedingly well—all right, let's not put it that I'm asking for your advice, let's say I'm asking out of sheer curiosity—if you were in my shoes, what would you do? Or is being in my shoes too utterly unthinkable?

It's perfectly thinkable, I said, we're very much alike in some ways. My dear Olly, said Patrick, you don't know how delighted I am to hear you say that! Why are you delighted? I asked. Because, said Patrick, it must mean that there's some hope for me, in the long run. No, tell me, Olly, in all seriousness and curiosity, what would you do?

How can I tell you, I said, when I don't know Tom at all? Never mind about Tom, said Patrick, let Tom equal X—or, if it makes this easier for you to understand, let Tom equal the sweetest, most attractive girl you care to imagine—the principle's the same.

In other words, I said, Tom himself isn't important? I never suggested that for a moment. (Patrick pretended to be quite indignant.) Of course I fully realize that he isn't important to *you*, he couldn't be, and besides you're very naturally prejudiced in the other direction. But I love Tom. You'll just have to take that on trust, incredible as it may seem to you. And I love Penny and Daphne and Deirdre with all my heart. You believe *that*, don't you?

The way Patrick seemed to be putting Tom on the same level as Penelope, that really jarred on me. I suppose he meant it to. It was probably from this point on that my tone started to get nasty. Does Penelope know about Tom, I asked him.

No, he said.

Are you planning to tell her? I asked.

When the right moment comes. But one never has to spell things out to Penny. If you try to, you always find that she's far ahead of you—she's so marvellously understanding. There's this thing between us—a kind of telepathy almost—the only danger is, one's apt to start taking it for granted and assume that other people have it too. I have to keep reminding myself how lucky I am. (Patrick made this all the more nauseating by saying it rather sacredly, as though it was something into which outsiders mustn't pry.)

Is Tom understanding about Penelope, I asked, or haven't you told him you're married?

Of course I've told him, said Patrick, giggling slightly. What do you take me for, some sneaking little bigamist with a double life?

Well, if both of them are so understanding, I said, I suppose it'll work out somehow.

Olly, now you're just making fun of me! Even you with your other-worldliness can't pretend to be as naïve as all that! Of course, as far as my duty is concerned, it's all towards Penny and the Children—

Then leave them, I said.

Patrick was sincerely staggered. *Leave Penelope!* You simply can't mean that!

If she and the Children only represent duty to you, I said, you ought to leave them. You'll have to support them anyway—that's the duty part of it. But to *live* with them out of duty, that's heartless. You'd much better go to Tom. Or are you afraid he might become a duty too?

You're full of surprises, said Patrick. One always forgets what a romantic you are, underneath. So you *do* think I'm unfit for Penny? You think I ought to leave her? Of course one has to accept your motives as being absolutely above suspicion, considering your way of life. Otherwise one might easily jump to certain conclusions—

Immediately after I'd made the remark about duty I'd felt ashamed of myself, it was so spiteful and cheap. If Patrick hadn't answered as he did, I'd have apologized at once. But now I flared up in that humiliatingly reflex way I do. If you suspect my motives, I told him, you ought not to discuss Penny with me at all—that is, if you really give a damn about her, which I'm beginning to doubt—(Here I cut myself short with a terrific effort. I was appalled by the state I was in.) Patrick, I said after a pause, please try to forget I said that. I'm sorry. Forgive me.

There's nothing to forgive, Patrick said, putting his hand on my arm for a moment. What you said happens to be untrue, but I'm glad you said it, Olly, I honestly am—because of the *way* you said it. Do you realize that this is the first time you've spoken to me frankly, I mean *really* frankly, since I've been here?

It was my turn to be staggered. I'm sure that Patrick knew how I felt, and that it pleased and amused him. He went on, in a tone of gentle, reproachful intimacy, do you know why I made such a point of coming here to see you, Olly—it was because I felt that perhaps you needed to talk to me, even if you weren't aware of it. I'll admit that there've been times while I've been here when I've felt pretty frustrated. It began to seem as if, after all, you wouldn't talk or *couldn't*. Look, I'm going to put my cards on the table, I'm going to make a confession to you. When I told you about Tom just now, I did that with a purpose. I mean, I could easily have made up some story to explain his behaviour, or simply laughed it off, or told you only part of the truth—I didn't have to tell you everything. But when Tom phoned I suddenly saw it was a heaven-sent opportunity to prove to you that I could be one-hundred-per-cent frank with you—

But Patrick, I said, what I don't understand is, *why* did you want to prove that to me? I should have thought that was obvious, said Patrick; I wanted to encourage you to be frank with me, too. I'm sorry, I said, but I still don't understand—what is there for me to be frank about?

Do you seriously want *me* to tell you? (Again I could hear that Patrick was grinning.) Of course I do, I said; but my voice was slightly shaky. Somewhere in the very midst of me, a feeling of uneasiness began to grow. I most certainly do, I said.

It'd only be the truth as I see it, Patrick said, and I may be monumentally wrong. Perhaps I ought to keep my mouth shut. I might only make you angry.

I want to hear it, I said. I won't be angry.

Oh, don't be alarmed. (Patrick laughed, he was thoroughly enjoying this, I could tell.) I'm not going to *accuse* you of anything. I hope you know how much I respect you—you're a far *better* person than I shall ever be. Not that that's saying much! No, seriously, I believe you're one of those very rare people who are literally incapable of being false—I mean *consciously* false. I really do believe that. I believe you've always acted

126

with complete sincerity and good faith, whatever you've done—I say, I don't think I'd better go on with this, had I?

I want you to go on, I said.

Oh hell, do you really? I'm already wishing I hadn't started! All right, here goes. Let me put it to you in this way: The one thing I'm concerned about is that I'm afraid you may be suffering from a very dangerous misunderstanding of yourself. If I'm right, it must have been influencing you and the decisions you've made for a long time now, perhaps ever since you grew up.

Does that include my decision to become a monk, I asked.

Oh, very much so—that most of all. As I say, I'm not for one instant questioning your good faith—Look, do you mind my telling you what I believe your real reason was for giving up your job with the Red Cross? You've explained all that to me, I know—how you met the Swami and gradually came to see things his way. I'm sure you believe in that explanation implicitly, but it's not the true one, at least not according to me. I believe your actual motive had nothing directly to do with your Swami—in fact, I'll even venture to suggest that it was *because* you had to find some rationalization for your urge to leave the Red Cross that you ever allowed yourself to listen to his teachings in the first place! Subconsciously, you must have been on the lookout for someone like him—you needed what he stood for *symbolically*. Perhaps, in the end, you might even have been forced to invent him, as it were—only, luckily for you, he actually existed. I mean, you had the amazing luck to meet this very remarkable and admirable individual, as he obviously *was*, instead of having to make do with some charlatan—*Please*, Olly, don't be angry with me! And don't just dismiss all this out of hand. Ask yourself if I'm not partly right—

127

I'm not angry, I said, and I'm not dismissing anything. Go on.

What you've *got* to admit to yourself, Olly—however much it may disturb you to do it—is that you're denying a very large part of your nature. Now isn't that the truth? You have powers that you absolutely refuse and *fear* to make use of. In your heart of hearts you know it, of course, you *must* know it—

You mean, I said, that I'd have made a better-than-average bank director?

I do not mean anything of the kind, and you know damn well I don't! I'll even concede that you made a very smart move when you walked out of that bank of yours. Oh, I know you did it from the loftiest motives—but I suspect you may have realized instinctively at the same time that it was the wrong kind of work for you—it would never have given you the scope you needed, even after you'd climbed to the top, as you undoubtedly would have. Now please understand, I'm *not* talking about executive ability, a talent for administration or whatnot—yes, you have that too, I don't doubt, but it's common enough these days, because it's what everyone's being trained for—you should just see them in the States, now—and to think Napoleon called *us* a nation of shopkeepers! Success of that sort is all very nice—it brings you in a lot of money and an illusion of importance—but when you have it you're still only a super-merchant. I ought to know, I'm one myself, and a good deal brighter than most of them—bright enough to know what I am and what I'm not and never can be. Don't underestimate your old brother, he's got a keen nose! I can smell this other thing a mile off—this thing I haven't got and no merchant can ever have—on the extremely few occasions when I meet it. That's what you've got, Oliver, whether you want it or not. It's a quality not more than perhaps three or four dozen people have in any given generation—the power to lead others and make them forget their own vanity and selfish interests and finally become almost noble. Everybody recognizes this power in wartime and adores it, but actually it's far more difficult to exercise in peacetime, when it's essentially much more impressive. In all seriousness, Oliver, I'm convinced that you could handle any kind of project you chose to take on, nothing would be too big for you. Of course it's possible you may lose this power by degrees, if you persist in denying its existence—

All this certainly sounds impressive, I said with a very unconvincing laugh. But even if it were remotely true, which I question, why on earth should this power of mine have made me so anxious to leave the Red Cross?

Because you felt guilty. You see, on the one hand, this sort of power is absolutely inseparable from ambition. On the other hand, anybody who has it must long to use it, by his very nature. A man like you wants to use it in a worthy cause, but that's still ambition, and ambition horrifies you. You think it's utterly evil under all circumstances, so you renounce it. You try to hide from it in the midst of humble communal tasks, first for the Quakers, then for the Red Cross. But even there you find yourself beginning to take over the leadership, such as it is—you can't resist your nature and the others all gladly acknowledge it—you're merely becoming a king-frog in an unnecessarily small pond. I saw you in action in the Congo, remember! When your guilt-pressure reaches a certain level, you leave them and fly for safety to your Swami, who promises to annihilate you entirely—ego and ambition and all.

But, Patrick, I objected, you haven't explained *why* I supposedly have this horror of ambition. Evidently **you** don't accuse the Swami of making me feel it, because you claim I had it long before I ever met him. I must say, I'm not aware of any horror, even nowadays—I mean, I'd never say that ambition was always wrong for everybody, at least within limits.

But *of course* you're not aware, Olly! How could you be? We're none of us aware of these deep compulsions. As to how you got it in the first place, I'm afraid I must blame Mother, entirely. She meant no harm, bless her! You can't even describe it as favouritism, though I used to resent her attitude before I began to understand it. She only did what so many mothers do—she cast her sons for roles in life, and they had to be different roles, of course, so that we shouldn't clash. I was to be the worldly success—that role was already taken before you appeared on the scene. So you were cast to be the unworldly one, the subtler, finer spirit who's above competition and shrinks from ambition in disgust as something vile and low. Poor old Olly! You were born to play one part, but Mother cast you for another! Don't you think it's time you took over your proper role? Don't you feel an obligation to use this power of yours? Have you the *right* to refuse to use it? Isn't this refusal ultimately selfish?

Suppose it is, I said. Suppose—just for the sake of argument—I do have this extraordinary thing you say I have, what do you propose I should do about it? Come on, Patrick, you've diagnosed my case, now let's hear your advice.

Advice? Really, Olly, who am *I* to presume to tell you?

You've told me quite a lot of things already, I said.

But that was all just theoretical, really.

Please be honest with me, Patrick, I said. You didn't mean it theoretically, I simply can't believe you did. Patrick, if you care for me at all, don't try to back out of it now, because this isn't something *I* can be theoretical about—it's my life. What you're actually telling me is that you think I oughtn't to be in this Monastery at all, isn't that it? I paused for him to answer, but he didn't. So I asked him, seriously—you think I ought to leave?

Oliver, I am *not* telling you that you *ought* or ought not to do anything—I want that to be clearly understood. Of course, if any of what I've said struck you as being true, I suppose you might just possibly come to a conclusion which would make leaving here the logical next step for you—

You mean leaving now, I said, at once, without taking sannyas?

I hardly see what your taking sannyas would prove, if you were intending to leave anyhow. I'm sure the Mahanta would release you from any obligation you may have to the Order. He's evidently a man of great understanding—

And what should I do then? I asked.

Oh, then your course of action would be perfectly clear. You'd fly straight back to England—I need hardly say that I'd be delighted to let you have whatever money you needed. I know a chap who could certainly find you something worthwhile, that'd really appeal to you, in the United Nations probably. And then in six months or a year, when they'd all realized what a treasure I'd dropped into their laps, they'd offer you one of the top jobs, something really *big*—

And what about my ambition? I said. A nerve in my left cheek had begun to twitch, something which hasn't happened to me once since I've been here. It used to twitch quite often when I was younger, whenever I got tense.

Oh, I think you'd soon stop bothering about your ambition, said Patrick. You'd learn not to be afraid of it when it had once been healthily satisfied.

You make the whole thing sound so simple, I said. All I have to do is write off everything that's happened in the last seven years.

My dear Oliver, this is your choice, not mine. If you should agree, on thinking this over, that you've been wrong about yourself, and if you should decide to change your life accordingly, then you'll know what's important to you and what isn't. Suppose you do decide that this Monastery, helpful as it may be for many kinds of people, is the wrong place for you to be in—a hiding-place from your natural vocation, in fact—that doesn't necessarily mean you'd have to give up believing in—sorry, I seem to have some block against remembering these Sanskrit names, I'm not even sure if it's a He or an It—

Just say God, I told him.

Thank you. I mean, speaking purely as an ignorant unbelieving outsider, I should have thought that if you really believed in God you'd actually be *proving* it by taking this plunge. You'd have proved to yourself that your faith was strong enough to survive, outside in the wicked world. I mean, I can quite well understand how the weaker brethren need the moral support of monastery walls and monastic rules and robes. But, heaven only knows, Olly, *you're* not weak!

I started laughing. My laughter was very near to hysteria, but Patrick didn't seem to notice this. He laughed too, in an ordinary way. And then his laugh turned into a big yawn. I'm afraid I've been talking an awful lot of rot, he said. I'm sorry, I suddenly feel most terribly sleepy. You've been very patient, listening to my ramblings. I'm afraid I've been keeping you up.

It was as if, without any warning, he'd slammed a door in my face. It left me completely frustrated and helpless. I wanted to beg him to stay with me, he seemed to have become the one person on earth who could decide my fate. I wanted to make him tell me what to do, or else unsay the things he'd said. And yet I couldn't speak to him, I couldn't even say goodnight. He said goodnight to me, and we parted, there on the spot.

I knew I shouldn't be able to sleep and I didn't even try to. I stayed out of doors, wandering around in the dark. I tried sitting on Swami's seat but even there I felt restless. I had to get up again and keep moving. The Temple was no good, either.

After what seemed like infinite ages, it got light. Then I forced myself to begin writing all this down. That seemed to be the only way of stopping my mind from running round and round in circles—now at least I've reviewed the whole thing consecutively from start to finish. I'd hoped that writing it down would help me to look at it objectively, but I already know that it hasn't. And though I've tired myself so that I'm shaking all over, I'm still a hundred miles from feeling sleepy.

One moment, everything that Patrick said seems utterly idiotic and even laughable. The next, it seems terribly insidiously true.

I feel like a madman—that's to say I have absolutely no idea what I may or may not do next.

To go to Patrick, tell him he was right and borrow the money from him for a ticket back to England—wouldn't that be the ultimate unthinkable humiliation? Yes. But, just because it's ultimate, it's not really unthinkable. In fact, I'm beginning to see it as the only thinkable act which wouldn't have even the least taint of falseness in it. All other ways of mortifying Oliver seem like self-cheating of one kind or another. But this one I can believe in, this would really strike Oliver's pride at its roots and bring him down grovelling to the ground. For that very reason it's appallingly attractive.

There's one insane thought which keeps recurring, I can't get it out of my head: When Patrick told me about himself and Tom, wasn't he implicitly offering me Penny?

Swami, I'm praying to you now as I've never prayed before. Show me what I must do.

7

My dear Tom,

    after our conversation last night, I feel I must get a letter off to you at once. You see, I'm terribly afraid that some of the things I said then may have hurt you. Of course, there's always the possibility that you don't remember what I did say—you certainly were drunk! But I can't count on that—I mean, I have no desire to count on it. I *want* you to remember, because this is something we have to get cleared up between us, in all frankness. (Perhaps you'll say to yourself, well, if he's in such a hurry to clear things up, why the hell doesn't he telephone me? But I think, if you do remember anything about last night, you'll have to agree that that just wouldn't be sensible. It would still be almost impossible for us two to communicate calmly with each other in our present emotional state. We'd only get excited and incoherent and tie ourselves up in further misunderstandings.)

First of all, I want to tell you that I do understand perfectly what made you make that call. (How on earth you managed to find out the number and get yourself put through to me is nothing short of a miracle. No wonder it took you most of the night!) Believe me, Tom, there've been many times when I longed to call *you*. I know only too well what loneliness can do to one—how, if one lets oneself brood on it, it distorts everything into a nightmare of isolation and self-pity, until one simply doesn't stop to consider the consequences of one's actions, or just doesn't care what they'll be. I know I lost my temper last night and said some things I shouldn't have said and didn't quite mean. But all the time I was saying them I felt so deeply *sorry,* sorry for you and sorry for myself.

I think very few of us ever take the trouble to visualize what may be going on at the other end of a telephone line. I know I often fail to do that myself, and sometimes one can't be expected to. How could you possibly have known that I was talking to you last night in the presence of at least thirty people, several of whom undoubtedly understood English quite well, well enough certainly to get a general idea of what was going on between us? The fact that our conversation was, to put it mildly, personal didn't mean to them that it should be private. No one left the room. I suppose in Asia this kind of insensitiveness, as it appears to be from our viewpoint, is normal behaviour, like not moving away when people pee in the street!

So I was rattled, I'm afraid, and all the more so because I knew you'd already spoken to my Brother. I don't know exactly what you said to him, he didn't tell me and I didn't ask him, but it was obvious that you'd been pretty hysterical, I saw that from his manner. I'm sure you didn't leave him in any doubt as to what the relations between you and me were. My Brother isn't by any means a prude, you mustn't imagine him as 'religious' in the American sense of the word, in fact he's wonderfully understanding, but still it wasn't very pleasant for me to have to confess to him everything that has gone on between us. I say 'confess,' because having to tell him outright like that, without any preparation, made it sound like a confession. But I owed it to him not to spare any details, because of course he may well have to face questions from his superiors, if they get to hear about our conversation from those who were present. I know that Oliver in his loyalty will do his best to cover up the whole affair and make light of it, even though, as a monk, he will be committing a grave sin by not telling the unvarnished truth. This will cause him great distress, I know, and most probably he'll punish himself for it later with severe self-inflicted penances. That's one of the aspects of this wretched business which makes me feel most ashamed—I've made my Brother's position here just that much more difficult. And it can't ever have been easy. As an Englishman who is trying desperately to be accepted as a fellow-monk and a Hindu, one of themselves, he must be under constant observation by the people in this Monastery. I don't doubt that there are a few malicious or chauvinistic ones who actually *hope* he'll fail to measure up to their standards. Imagine what they'll make out of this scandal, if they get the chance!

I don't give a damn about myself, of course. I shall be leaving this place anyhow in three days at the most, and I'll certainly never be coming back here, I couldn't possibly, after what's happened. I am only thinking of my Brother. No, that's not quite true—I'm thinking also of the elder monks, the ones I've met and got to know. They've been so extraordinarily kind to me, and I should hate it if they should be told about this. It's all very well to be defiant and say that my private life is my own affair. Yes, that's true, but only as long as I keep it private. By letting it become public I force my standards of behaviour on them, as it were—and what right have I to do that? They never preached to me, never tried to make me conform, never forced their monk-hood on me in any way. I feel I've abused their hospitality. And that I hate. That's really humiliating.

All the same, I shouldn't have been angry with you.

How could you have understood any of this? You are an impulsive creature, Tommy dear, as you well know, and that's a great part of your charm. You're spontaneous and reckless and you absolutely refuse to look ahead. I'm just beginning to realize how awfully young you are, young even for your age. Since last night I see that we do actually belong to two different generations. I suppose that's a fact of life which I ought to have faced from the start and which my vanity stopped me from facing! While we were together you helped me avoid facing it, because most of the things you wanted us to do together were physical and we could still be equals physically—I haven't yet begun to fall apart at the seams!

But seriously, though, the realization of how young you are emotionally was the greatest shock I got from last night. It has made me think very hard. I begin to see our relationship in an altogether different light, and for the first time I feel guilty about it, because I now see that I involved you in something which was far out of your depth.

I wrote in my last letter about our facing the world together. I see now how utterly monstrously selfish my attitude was. I told you that you were my one chance of becoming alive and really living, and that was certainly true—my God, you'll never dream how true it was! I know you'd have given me everything I asked for, all of yourself that you had to give. But that doesn't mean I'd have had the right to accept it. I don't have that right— that's what I've understood, just in time, before it's too late.

The fact that you must try to accept, Tommy dear, is that you and I could never have been happy together, no matter how much courage and determination and good luck we might have had. It's not that my feelings for you aren't as strong as yours for me—perhaps mine

138

are even stronger—but the point is, they're of two very different kinds. You see, my feelings are based on a clear objective critical knowledge of you. Yes, I do think I can claim to know you pretty thoroughly, even after this short friendship. But, Tom, do you know *me* even a little? I very much fear that the person you think you know is quite largely a creation of your own desires and fantasies. He's not even altogether disentangled from that absurd character Lance in the novel you gave me! He seems glamorous to you because he has travelled in foreign countries you think of as exotic, and known certain famous people you think you'd love to know, and had experiences you imagine you'd give anything to have. What you can't possibly understand is his attitude to all of this. I'm not saying that it's entirely cynical and world-weary—a few, a very few, of the people and experiences *were* worth the effort—but it is quite different from yours. And if you don't understand my attitude to my past life, how can you claim to know *me?*

Oh, it was all my fault, of course. In my eagerness to seem young to you, I instinctively concealed my oldness of spirit, my tiredness. That wasn't too difficult, because these things don't show on the outside yet. But they are there inside me. You see, I have been hurt, I don't want to remember how many times, there's no sense in brooding over it. You don't know what it's like, thank goodness, that kind of disappointment in someone which takes the edge off your faith in life—blunts it, so to speak, only a little perhaps, but it can never be quite the same again.

You gave me back some of my faith, as much as *could* be given back, and I'll be everlastingly grateful to you for that. The only way I can repay you is to make sure that you won't ever be disillusioned by me. Somebody will hurt you sooner or later, I'm afraid, because you're so reckless and innocent and loving—but it won't be me, that I can prevent, at any rate.

For God's sake, don't get the suspicion that this is leading up to some dishonest attempt to say goodbye without actually saying it, just to spare your feelings and save me embarrassment! I give you my word, I'll be your friend always—one of your truest friends, I hope. And of course we shall meet again. Only I do think we need a period of separation first, probably quite a long one. We ought not to see each other again until we can take each other more lightly. I think we got off on the wrong foot. Our relationship was so dramatic and desperate—sometimes rather ridiculously so. Don't you agree?

Dearest Tommy, I'm well aware that what I've written may upset you, to begin with, but I'm confident that you'll come to agree that I was right—and then perhaps you'll even be grateful to me. If you feel deserted and deprived, please remind yourself that it's really I who am giving up and losing far more than you are. I'm losing *you!* I'm saying goodbye—I mean, as a lover—to probably the last and certainly the sweetest and sexiest boy I shall ever have had in my life. As long as my poor old nerves can even twitch, I'll remember the feel of you in my arms. They can never take that away from me. And, no matter who takes my place with you, at least I'll always be able to say I was there before him!

Yes, I *do* wish you another lover, someone altogether more suitable, closer to your own age, with more faith and courage and innocence than I had left to give you. I hope you'll find that having been with me has done something to help you be happy with him. I'll imagine the two of you together sometimes—yes, even on that rock at Tunnel Cove! I give you both my blessing in advance—and I'm already as jealous as hell!

As for me, well, there'll always be my work. I must

plunge back into that. And then there's my family—I have my duty to them, and one of the chief things I can count on to keep me going is that they have so many needs which it's up to me to satisfy, in a practical way. Duty often seems to me to be the only thing one can really count on, in the long run. Happiness may be thrown in as an occasional bonus, but one never knows how long it will last.

I won't write again until I've heard from you that you've received this letter. I have to know, first, how you'll react to it. *Please*, don't sit down the moment you've read it and scribble off something impulsive and violent! Don't reply for twenty-four hours at least. First read it carefully several times and think it over even more carefully.

About those letters which are already waiting for me in Singapore—Tom, I am not going to read them. That would be just rubbing salt into the wound, and it doesn't seem fair to you. So I'll either burn them unopened or send them back to you—let me know which you prefer. In any case, I beg you, burn all *my* letters, for your own sake! If you keep them around and reread them, they'll only make you unhappy. Rather than that, I'd much prefer you to get furious with me, if it helps!

And now I can say something I could never say before—I love you, and I always shall. And that includes being *in love* with you. I know in my bones that I'll still be a little bit in love with you on my hundredth birthday, which I fully intend to celebrate! I'm not asking you to go on being in love with me—I wouldn't even want that—but please don't ever forget your

Patrick.

Wait—I haven't finished yet!

All the time I've been writing this letter, something has kept nagging at me which I feel I ought to say to you. I hesitate to say it because I'm so afraid you may misunderstand, and yet I know I absolutely must. If I really wish you well, and I do with all my heart, then I have *no right* to keep my mouth shut.

Tom, when I refer above to your future lover, I seem to take it for granted that the lover will be a he. That's an impression I want to correct. Look—are you *absolutely* sure you can't have a relationship with a girl? I know you told me you'd tried it two or three times, but that was back in high-school, wasn't it, and they may merely have been the wrong ones for you. I think you do at least know me well enough to know that I'd never dream of suggesting you should go against your nature. But when someone is—as you must admit you are— such a militant standard-bearer in the ranks of the man-lovers, isn't it just possible that his sexual inclinations may be partly prejudice? Steady now, don't start denying this right away! First ask yourself frankly, am I against heterosexual love simply because it's respectable and legal and approved of by the churches and the newspapers and all those other vested interests I hate?

Sometimes I've worried about you, Tommy, fearing that you'll waste much of your wonderful vitality in defying organized Society—such a hopeless fruitless occupation! Society itself couldn't care less, and that kind of defiance only hardens and embitters the defier in the long run and makes him old before his time. We can't have that happening to *you*, can we? If you honestly don't like girls, you don't—all I'm urging is that you should give them a few more tries. They *do* have their advantages, you know, the chief of which is that they can provide you with children. You of all people, with so much love to give, ought not to miss the marvellous experience of being a father. I can promise you that becoming a husband is a very small price to pay for it!

Being married does make a lot of things easier, because the world accepts marriage at its face value, without asking what goes on behind the scenes—whereas it's always a bit suspicious of bachelors! The unmarried are apt to regard marriage as a prison—actually it gives you much greater freedom. And you'd be amazed how many of the married men I know personally swing both ways. Some of them will even admit that they feel more at ease making love with other married men, rather than with out-and-out homosexuals, whom they're inclined to look on as somewhat wilful freaks.

May I also call to your attention that one of your best-seller American psychologists—I forget his name, but I once came across a paperback of his at your place, it must have enraged you if you ever read it—maintains that man is bisexual by nature and that the homosexual who rigidly rejects women under all circumstances is being just as unnatural and *square* as the heterosexual who rejects men!

Enough said! Now, Tommy dear, *do* try to keep an open mind toward whatever the future may bring you and *don't* dismiss it out of hand if it happens to be wearing a skirt!

It's less than eight hours since I last wrote in this diary, and yet the whole world seems changed. This time I have no scruples about breaking my resolve—in fact I'm not breaking it. The reasons for making the resolve are no longer valid. And I must record exactly what has happened while it's still fresh in my mind.

I know it would be perfectly proper for me to tell Mahanta Maharaj about this, but I'm not going to, at least not yet. This is something so extremely personal to me that I want to keep it to myself for a while. Maharaj would understand it perfectly, of course, but in his different, Hindu way. He wouldn't quite see what it means to me, and there are aspects of it which I couldn't very well explain to him. Anyhow, Swami often used to tell me that it's dangerous, especially for a beginner, to describe such things to other people, because one may so easily lapse into indirect bragging.

About an hour ago, in the middle of this afternoon, I was standing outside our sleeping-quarters in the courtyard, leaning against a small tree. I was dazed with tiredness but still unable to sleep and still in the violently disturbed state I was in this morning, not knowing what on earth to do next. I leaned with my back against the tree trunk and closed my eyes, feeling as if I had absolutely no strength left to make a movement in any direction. I suppose, half consciously, I was still praying to Swami for help.

Sleep must have hit me very suddenly. I don't even remember lying down. Perhaps I was already asleep when my legs sagged and I slid to the ground, where I found myself when I woke. This sleep was wonderfully deep and refreshing, but brief—it can't have lasted more than half an hour. Presumably it was a few moments before waking that I saw Swami.

Yes, I can say I did literally see him, although this wasn't a vision in the waking state. But seeing him was only a part of the experience of his presence, which was intensely vivid, far more so than an ordinary dream. Also, unlike a dream, it didn't altogether end when I woke up. It is losing strength now, but it's still going on inside me at this moment.

I can't say where it took place—*where* is a meaningless word in this connection, anyway—it could have been in Swami's flat in Munich or it could have been here, it wasn't specifically either. In one sense it was here rather than in Munich, because it had such a feeling of being absolutely *now*.

I was with Swami from the beginning, I mean he

didn't appear to me at a certain moment, I simply became aware that we were together—and it didn't seem as if we had only just met. We were domestically together as we used to be in the old days. Swami was sitting cross-legged on a bed or couch—the room was nondescript and not recognizable—and I was making tea for him, boiling water in a kettle on a gas-ring. I felt happy and at peace, as I always used to be while doing him any small service. In that sense, we did seem to be back in Munich.

At the same time, I was quite clearly aware that Swami was already 'dead'—that's to say no longer in his earthly body. And I understood, in a way I'd never understood before, that making this tea for him was both physically unnecessary and spiritually of tremendous importance. It was a symbolic act, but it was every bit as important as making tea that would actually be drunk, or indeed doing any other kind of physical service, for an embodied being. The spiritual significance was all that ultimately mattered, and it was the same in either case. In other words, I really and deeply understood, at long last, what Swami used to keep trying to teach me and what I used to repeat after him so glibly without any true understanding, about the symbolic nature of all action.

I knew that Swami was 'dead', and I knew that nevertheless he was now with me—*and that he is with me always, wherever I am*. While he was in the body, he wasn't always with me, that's obvious. If I was away at work, we could only be together in our thoughts, at best. But now we are never separated. I woke up actually *knowing* that. I can't say that I still know it, in that absolute sense, as I write these words, but at least I can still vividly remember how I felt at the time. My eyes keep filling with tears of joy, remembering it.

And now I come to the thing which is hardest to de-

145

all actions are
symbolic—

scribe, because it's so strange. All the time that Swami and I were together, we were communicating with each other—I hesitate to say 'talking' because I have no memory of a single word we said. Perhaps the communication was nonverbal and telepathic. In any case, what we were communicating about was Patrick.

While Swami and I were living together he very seldom asked me about my past life or the members of my family. Of course I had told him at the beginning about Patrick and Penelope and the Children and Mother, but not very much. They seemed far away from our life, and there was almost never a reason for me to mention any of them. Swami can only have had the vaguest picture of what they were like.

But now it seemed to me that Patrick was very close to us—in the next room, as it were. And I was aware that he was an established part of our life, the three of us belonged together intimately and I accepted this as a matter of course. There was no question of my feeling any jealousy or hostility towards him—in that situation such feelings were unimaginable.

Swami seemed quietly but gravely concerned about Patrick. He was like a doctor discussing the condition of a very sick patient—only what he was discussing was Patrick's spiritual, not physical condition. And yet, despite his gravity and concern, he seemed amused and even on the verge of smiling—shaking his head over Patrick, so to speak, with an air of indulgent amusement, as if to say, 'Oh my goodness, what *will* he be up to next?' The general impression I had was that Patrick had got himself into a spiritual state which was very serious, so serious as to be almost ridiculous, but that nevertheless *he would be all right*.

That's all I have to record. It's quite beside the point to try to guess how long the experience lasted. It didn't need time, or hardly any, because it didn't progress or change, it was simply a situation. There were just these three aspects of the situation and they remained constant throughout it—Swami's presence, my tea-making, Swami's concern about Patrick.

This much I'm sure of, Swami wouldn't have revealed his concern for Patrick to me without a purpose. It can't be that he wants me to help Patrick in any way, for what other help does Patrick need if Swami is with him? So this must be an admonition to me, for my own sake—that I'm to try to remember always, from this moment on, that Patrick is in Swami's care and in Swami's presence—even though he himself may be utterly unaware of it now and for some time to come.

Sooner or later, certainly, Patrick *will* become aware of it, either gradually or suddenly. Suppose Swami appears to him, as he has to me—how would Patrick react to the experience? Wouldn't he have to persuade himself that it was 'just a dream'? But I mustn't make such assumptions. Who am I to dare to say what the power that works through Swami can do? I only know that it would be terribly wrong for me to tell Patrick that I know this about him—not that it would make any particular difference if I did tell him, because he'd never believe me. But it would be wrong for me to meddle.

But now another thought occurs to me. I have allowed myself to get frantically upset by Patrick's being here, and have even felt that he was challenging my whole way of life by his mere presence. That wasn't all my imagination, either—last night he as good as urged me to walk out of this Monastery and give up being a monk. What I haven't asked myself until this moment is, *Why did he do that?* And now I believe I have the answer.

I've always taken it for granted that Patrick has never felt any dissatisfaction with *his* way of life, and I'm sure that used to be true. But I suspect that now he has begun to feel dissatisfied—it probably began quite recently—and that that's the reason why he wants me to stop being a monk. If I left the Order he'd take it as a reassurance that his way of life was the right one, and that all possibility of another kind of life, with quite different aims and values, could be dismissed as self-deception and nonsense.

Now, why has Patrick started to feel like this? What, actually, *is* his dissatisfaction? Couldn't it be the first faint beginning of an awareness that some new and unknown power is working inside him? Couldn't he be starting to be aware of Swami's presence? That would surely be a most disconcerting sensation for him at first. It would make him increasingly dissatisfied with everything he used to think was desirable and important, and he wouldn't even know why!

No wonder Swami seemed amused! If you look at this objectively, it's a pretty comic situation. Poor old Paddy—he's in a state of grace! And he's going to discover it the hard way. He doesn't dream what he's in for, but he'll find out before long.

Oh, Penny—

I don't think I have ever felt a greater need to write to you than I do now—there's so much I want to say.

Actually, I'm not going to post this letter until I get to Singapore. It should reach you quicker from there than it would from here, and I'll be there tomorrow evening—no, *this* evening, it's long past midnight already. But I want to write now, while I'm still here, rather than tomorrow while I'm on the plane. Whatever may be said against this place—and I *have* said a good deal, haven't I?—it does seem to create an atmosphere in which you can think your thoughts more objectively and indeed almost look at them while you're thinking them. I have a strange, rather exhilarating feeling that I've never understood certain things about myself and my life as clearly as I do at this moment. I'm afraid life will begin to appear in its usual complex muddle as soon as I return to a more normal environment.

Another reason for writing this letter now, a very secondary one, is that I have got to do *something* to keep me awake! This is Olly's great night—the night of sannyas, during which he actually becomes a swami. The ceremony must have begun by this time, and it's scheduled to last until dawn, and for some funny reason I feel I ought not to go to bed, I want to hold my own little private vigil to keep him company! Do you think that's idiotic of me? Whether it is or not, nobody but you will ever know about it. Even if I do manage not to drop off to sleep, I can't possibly tell Olly what I've done—he might so easily misunderstand and think I was somehow making mock of this sacred occasion.

One of the swamis explained a bit about the significance of the rituals to me—he did this when I asked him what had become of Olly, whom I haven't seen for the past three days. It seems that, before you take sannyas, you have to go through a preliminary ceremony called the shraddha, a sort of funeral service. You perform rites in advance for the peace of your parents' souls because, as a monk, you won't be able to do this when your parents actually do die—monks aren't supposed to take part in any rites connected with birth, marriage or death, they're trained to regard all three as mere aspects of illusion! After you've done this you perform similar rites for yourself, signifying that you are now 'dying to the world'. This shraddha service was held in the morning of the day before yesterday, and Olly has remained incommunicado since then because —having died as himself and not yet been reborn as a swami—he's been technically a spook!

(I can't help laughing when I think how hideously gruesome and morbid Mother would find all this— particularly the idea that Olly has, so to speak, buried her before her time!)

I keep picturing him over there now in the Temple, not five minutes' walk from this room and yet so far removed from me and from all of us—so far from home! Nevertheless, he *is* still our own Olly, ridiculously British, hopelessly out of his element, muffled in those alien robes and mumbling the words of that dead language, amongst all those dark faces. I find this act of his, the sheer courage of it, terribly moving. He's so utterly, almost unimaginably alone in what he's doing—far more so than any lone hero on a battlefield. Mind you, it still fills me with a certain horror and one does feel it's a ghastly waste, even if the waste is heroic, a sort of spiritual Charge of the Light Brigade—c'est magnifique, mais ce n'est pas la vie!

Still, I'm not really concerned about Olly's future. I feel sure now that nothing is going to defeat him, in the long run. People with his kind of strength work out their own destinies almost in spite of themselves, no matter what perverse disciplines and rules they insist on observing. However much Olly may try to persuade himself that he believes in humility, obedience and anonymity, he's actually quite incapable of remaining a holy nobody. I believe he's going to make something extraordinary out of being a swami, something peculiarly his own.

The other night I at length found an opportunity to speak to him about himself, and very frankly. I don't know how much of an impression I made, there were moments when I thought I was getting through to him, but then I seemed to lose contact again. I suppose in any case it was much too late in the game to expect any immediate results.

But what I'm beginning to wonder is if I didn't make an utter fool of myself, talking to him like that. There I was, pleading with him not to desert us, not to hide himself in a crowd of Hindus but come back and help us in the West, where he belonged. I even suggested he should take a job with some agency of the United Nations! But now I wonder, in making plans like that for him, wasn't I aiming far too low?

The wild idea has suddenly struck me that Olly may fulfil his real destiny by staying in this country, by staying on in this Monastery even—at least for the present. Perhaps his destiny *is* to be a foreigner. They say that this part of Asia is intensely nationalistic and skin-conscious, nowadays—but a situation like that always means that there's a throne vacant for the extraordinary outsider, the paleface prophet. Perhaps Olly, by virtue of his foreignness, plus of course his Hinduism and monastic status, will gradually evolve into one of those terrifyingly uncorrupt politico-religious leaders who appear from time to time to be adored by millions, dominate international conferences and finally checkmate the opposition by getting themselves assassinated! Perhaps that ass Rafferty, with the genius of his unspeakable vulgarity, has actually had a true glimpse of what Olly will become! If he turns out to have been right, won't that be a laugh on the rest of us—and on Olly most of all?

Dear old awe-inspiring preposterous Olly—however far His Holiness may choose to withdraw himself from *me*, I don't care, I feel so close to *him* tonight! And through him, I seem closer than ever to you, my darling —I mean, I feel such closeness in the thought of us three together. Each one of us will belong to the other two always, even if we never set eyes on Olly again. Do you know, while I've been with him here, I've often found myself wondering what would have happened if he had married you! We have never discussed you, only referred to you and the Children occasionally, and yet, oddly enough, I now know for certain that he's still in love with you. And you once told me that you were still in love with him. Isn't it strange that I can talk about this and not feel jealous? Oh, Penny, how extraordinary men and women are in their dealings with each other! Why do two people choose to live together, 'forsaking all others'? Is it love or need? Is the need to be needed stronger than love? Or does love, in its pure absolute (as in alcohol) form, need no relationships? Do we love

Olly because he doesn't need us? I know I need you. I hope to God you need me.

What is a 'marriage' anyway? I'm at my most natural with you, and we live as man and wife in every accepted meaning of the phrase, and yet as soon as I think of myself as a 'married man' I see that this isn't my natural role and that the word 'marriage' doesn't at all describe the most essential part of our life together. It seems to me that we only play at 'marriage' for the benefit of other people, to reassure them that we're like they are and not freaks. But why do we have to reassure them? Do we really care what they think of us? No, of course we don't. (I sometimes get the odd feeling that one gives out this reassurance as a sort of public service—lest some individual should be seized by the fear that he's the only non-freak in a world of freaks, and thus start a chain-reaction of panic leading to mass stampede and slaughter!) Even being parents is a game to us, isn't it? And yet I'm willing to bet that the Two Ds, when they grow up, will agree that they would much rather have had us than the genuine articles!

All the same, game-playing can be dangerous, because one may get to take it seriously. There *is* a danger that even you and I might start believing that I really *am* your husband! And there have been times, I know, when you have suddenly felt insecure, in spite of all your marvellous power of understanding, and begun to wonder if perhaps the game was reality after all. You've accepted the world's values and allowed yourself to think in terms of 'husband', 'wife', 'married couple', etc., and therefore told yourself that you were being humiliated, betrayed and so forth, because that's what married couples are supposed to do to each other. As if *I* could ever 'betray' *you!* I know I have hurt you sometimes, darling, though I've never meant to. When I did so unintentionally, it was because I simply couldn't believe I had the power to hurt you—I couldn't take myself seriously in that way, I mean, as a 'betrayer'!

Penny dearest, for the sake of our whole future together, I appeal to you—accept me as I am. Will you try to do that? Will you let me be silly sometimes, and show me you know it's only silliness and doesn't matter to you? Let me run off now and then, looking for my teen-age self and flexing my muscles! I can promise you one thing, I shall always return from these idiotic adventures with increased love for you and gratitude—in fact, I can only enjoy the adventures if you'll sanction them! Oh Penny, can't we forget about 'marriage' altogether and live in our own special way, the way that's natural to us? Can't I quite shamelessly be the child who keeps running home to you, and who is always thinking of you even in the midst of his play? When I see us in that relationship it's obvious to me that you can be more central to my life than any mere wife could be to any mere husband. Oh, it's all so beautifully simple, really —if only you can accept me *fully*, then you'll see how happy we shall be! Everything will be out in the open, happy and innocent, without lies or suspicions. And you'll be *everything* to me, without any rivals, even imaginary ones.

It's just conceivably possible that a young American named Tom, whom I met while I was in Los Angeles, may try to get in touch with you. *Please* don't let this upset you. He's terribly disturbed, poor boy, and terribly young, and because (I don't want to conceal anything from you, even when it's totally unimportant) we'd had a little interlude of pleasure together, he jumped to conclusions and imagined, I don't exactly know what, that I had somehow committed myself to him. As I say, he's disturbed and hysterical and given, as many hysterics are, to the very anti-social vice of long-distance telephoning! So he *might* try to make some kind of a scene with you and perhaps pretend that I've promised him all sorts of things which I never did or could have. If this happens, I'm sure you'll know how to cope with him. I shall never forget how understanding but firm you were with that poor tiresome child from Stockholm. (You see, I've even forgotten his name!)

As a matter of fact, this Tom did create quite a disturbance by phoning me *here*, and I've been forced to write him a very firm letter breaking the whole thing off, or rather, explaining that there really never was a 'thing' to break.

I am all yours, Penny. Yours and the Children's. Never doubt this. To me you are safety and freedom, both together, and those are the two things I need more than anything else in the world. Only you can give them to me.

Oh my darling, how I long for the Two Ps and the Two Ds to be reunited! I'll cut this business in Singapore as short as I can, and hurry home. I feel a new life is starting for us.

Yours sleepily but completely,
Paddy

Dearest Mother,

    forgive this long silence—it must be all of ten days since I last wrote. Well, anyhow, I now have something really exciting to write about, a piece of stop-press headline news—at approximately six a.m. this morning, Oliver became a swami!

Actually, of course, this process of becoming a swami consists of several ceremonies which take place over a period of days. For instance, the candidate for sannyas has first to be invested with the sacred thread, to signify that he has become a member of the caste of the Brahmins, which is the highest of all the castes. You might say that it's rather like being knighted or raised to the peerage, and the idea behind it is that if you're going to renounce earthly rank and fame you ought first to have something really worthwhile to renounce! There is also a beautiful ritual in which the candidate lays his former self to rest—thereby becoming a pure disembodied spirit—as a prelude to assuming his new monastic identity. I have carefully written down the name Oliver will have as a swami, but it's in a notebook in my bag, and I find I have forgotten it—the name, I mean! These Sanskrit names all sound rather alike to English ears, as they all end with the suffix -ananda, which means 'bliss' —in a spiritual sense, of course.

Later in the morning, Oliver and his newly-made fellow-swamis had to go out into the surrounding district and beg alms, just as Hindu monks have done for thousands of years. But in modern times—in this Order at any rate—the swamis only have to beg during their first three days. It's more of a symbolic thing really. I was in the Mahanta's room, saying goodbye to him, when Oliver returned with the food he had been given. He offered some of it to the Mahanta, and then he offered me some, which I thought was very touching. I felt that Oliver did this to make it clear that he wasn't disowning me or excluding me from his new life—and of course that applied equally to you and Penny.

He wasn't able to come with me to the airport, but we had a short walk in the grounds before I left. As we walked, people kept running forward and bending to touch his feet, which were bare, in token of their reverence! It was really beautiful, the way Olly took this. He smiled shyly and raised his hands palm to palm, touching them to his forehead with a bashful deprecatory gesture. He looked even taller than usual, among all the little Bengalis, wonderfully handsome and every inch a holy man, with the long flame-coloured robe falling to his feet. You would have been proud of him I know, and happy to see how well he seems suited to his new role in life. I was so proud to walk beside him and know that everybody knew he was my brother.

Incidentally, the Mahanta told me that a monk, when he takes his final vows, gains liberation for his entire family—so you and Penny and the Children, and even I, need never worry about the health of our souls again, thanks to Olly! I shall try not to take unfair advantage of this immunity—though I must admit, it creates a temptation!

Am writing this on the plane to Singapore. We shall be there in another hour.

Ever lovingly,
Paddy

Did Oliver die? No and Yes. I see now I was silly to expect some melodramatic transformation. Now I understand that the dying and being reborn are a gradual process. Nevertheless, since this morning, the process has truly begun and that's all that matters. I feel absolutely confident—sooner or later, through Swami's grace, Oliver will die.

Sannyas is far more than taking vows; it's entering into freedom. While I was out begging with the others this morning, I felt utterly free—as I hope to become increasingly—from the burden of being Oliver. So, for the first time, there were no barriers between us, I wasn't an alien, and the others seemed to understand this, we kept smiling and laughing for no special reason. I'm not saying this in self-pity but in amazement—up to today I'd lived my life without once knowing what it really meant, to be happy.

I love the begging. We have to do it barefoot. Mahanta Maharaj told me I could wear sandals if I wanted to, but of course I didn't. My feet hurt a bit, but I'm glad I didn't toughen them up beforehand, because the slight discomfort keeps reminding me of the significance of what I'm doing.

You don't beg primarily for yourself, but for the Mahanta as head guru and the senior swamis of the Order. Remembering this made it easier to accept the alms in the right spirit—whole families bowing down with such simple devotion. You mustn't even say to yourself, I'm not worthy. You mustn't take it personally at all. I brought back what I'd been given, a mess of

158

runny tepid food in the fold of my cloth, and offered it to Maharaj and the rest of them. Patrick gallantly ate some, though I could see he nearly gagged on it!

When he left for the airport we were quite formal with each other and shook hands and murmured some conventional leave-taking phrases. But that didn't matter because we'd already had this other wonderful moment together which I shall remember always.

It was when we all came trooping out of the Temple at the end of the sannyas ceremony. That *was* like returning from the dead—I felt a sort of dazed joyful strangeness. A small crowd was waiting for us to appear, and Patrick was among them. My heart jumped when I saw him, I was so pleased. I'd never dreamed he would trouble to get up that early.

Everybody was watching us, to see how we'd behave. And of course I couldn't help being just a little bit embarrassed and self-conscious, standing there confronting him in my brand-new gerua. He came towards me smiling, with his camera-case slung around his neck. As he walked he took the camera out of it, and when he was within a few feet of me he stopped and quickly snapped off half a dozen pictures. I felt foolish, but I realized that he had to do this, to show the Family.

Then Patrick put his camera away and suddenly without any warning he dropped to his knees and took the dust of my feet and bowed down before me! He must have been rehearsing this, he did it so smoothly and neatly. In the midst of my astonishment, I was aware of a strong favourable reaction from the audience. Once again, Patrick's instinct had been absolutely correct, he had done the dramatically perfect thing! So then I hastily grabbed him by the shoulders and dragged him to his feet and hugged him. I did this to cover an uncontrollable attack of giggles—I was shaking with it, and as I held him I felt him beginning to laugh, too. His lips just touched my ear in a sort of kiss and he whispered, 'Well Olly, you've *really* gone and torn it now!' And I whispered back, 'Looks like I'm stuck with it, doesn't it?'

At that moment I seemed to stand outside myself and see the two of us, and Swami, and the onlookers, all involved in this tremendous joke. I felt Swami's presence with us so intensely that I was afraid I would begin sobbing with joy and tell Patrick everything. So I pushed him away from me and stepped back. The others took this as a sign that it was now all right for them to approach us. And everybody was smiling and murmuring, as much as to say how charming it was of Patrick to play this scene according to our local Hindu rules, and how very right and proper it was that we two brothers should love each other.